THE CLUE IN
THE PATCHWORK QUILT

A JUDY BOLTON Mystery

The Clue in the Patchwork Quilt

BY
Margaret Sutton

Illustrated by Pelagic Doane

APPLEWOOD BOOKS
Bedford, Massachusetts

eC 7/78
14.95
JF
8/08

The Clue in the Patchwork Quilt
was originally published in 1941.

Reprinted by permission of the estate of Margaret Sutton.
All Rights Reserved.

For a complete list of titles in the Judy Bolton Mysteries,
please visit judybolton.awb.com.

Thank you for purchasing an Applewood Book.
Applewood reprints America's lively classics—books from
the past that are still of interest to modern readers.
For a free copy of our current catalog, write to:

Applewood Books
P.O. Box 365
Bedford, MA 01730
www.awb.com

ISBN 978-1-4290-9034-6

MANUFACTURED IN THE U.S.A.

A MAN STEPPED OUT OF THE CAR AND JUDY
RECOGNIZED BLACKIE.

The Clue in the Patchwork Quilt   *Frontispiece (Page 157)*

A JUDY BOLTON MYSTERY

THE CLUE IN THE PATCHWORK QUILT

BY

MARGARET SUTTON

Author of
THE HAUNTED ATTIC
THE NAME ON THE BRACELET, etc.

ILLUSTRATED BY

PELAGIE DOANE

GROSSET & DUNLAP
PUBLISHERS   NEW YORK

To My Sister

WHO GAVE ME THE MEMORY QUILT
AND IN LOVING MEMORY OF

My Mother

WHO LEFT IT UNFINISHED

JUDY BOLTON
MYSTERY STORIES
By MARGARET SUTTON

★ ★ ★ ★ ★

CONTENTS

THE CLUE IN THE PATCHWORK QUILT

CHAPTER I

A Strange Encounter

It was a cold morning in March. The roads were slippery and Peter Dobbs had to drive carefully as he turned out of Roulsville and took the less familiar highway toward Emporium. With him in the front seat was Judy Bolton, her gray eyes much more solemn than usual.

"Peter," she said suddenly, "I forgot to order flowers."

"Your grandmother won't miss them," Peter said.

"I know," Judy agreed. "I don't like too many flowers at a funeral either. But there should be enough to—to show that people care. There weren't too many at Grandpa's funeral. It was dignified, the way he would have wanted it. And Grandma's is going to be the same way. Did I tell you that Miss Leonard has promised to sing *Lead Kindly Light?* It was Grandma's favorite hymn."

"Miss Leonard?" questioned Peter. "Is she

1

the reason why we're driving to Emporium?''

"Yes, you know her," Judy told him. "She used to sing in the choir in the old River Street church where we went when we were children. She lives in Emporium now and teaches music in the public schools. I told Mother we'd call for her. She couldn't have come to the funeral, otherwise, and she was one of Grandma's dearest friends."

"Only a friend? I always thought she was a relative," Peter said.

"She isn't—exactly. Horace and I used to call her Aunt Linda, but we never dared say it to her face, for fear of hurting her feelings. You see, Peter," Judy explained, "she would have been our aunt if Uncle John hadn't been killed in the last war. They were engaged and it nearly broke her heart. That was over twenty years ago, but she's never forgotten him and she's always treated us like relatives."

"Rather romantic, wasn't it?" agreed Peter. "I'll bet you wouldn't be that true to me."

"You're not going to get killed, I hope."

"I've been hoping that for the last half hour," Peter remarked as he surveyed the icy road. White fields stretched at either side and the usually busy highway out of Roulsville was now quite deserted. But presently a glass-topped greenhouse came in sight. Peter stopped the car and helped Judy out.

"We still have time to order flowers—" he began.

But Judy was standing beside him, motionless, staring at the yellow farmhouse beyond.

"Why, it's Sam Tucker's place!" she exclaimed. "My grandparents and I often came here. Grandpa was helping Sam Tucker with his haying the day of the Roulsville flood. You remember, this house wasn't touched when the dam broke and flooded the rest of the town, because it is so far up on the hillside."

"And you were staying with your grandparents above the dam. Judy, I'll never forget what a tragedy that flood might have been if it hadn't been for you and your brother——"

"Mostly my brother," Judy interrupted. "Thinking of Grandpa and Grandma brings it all back, doesn't it?"

"Indeed it does. Well, Sam Tucker ought to remember us," said Peter as he pushed open the greenhouse door.

Judy took a deep breath of the warm fragrant air that rushed out against her face. There was no one in the greenhouse and they stood there a moment, puzzled. Should they walk around to the house or was there a bell they could ring? But presently a little white terrier came trotting out from behind a clump of plants and announced them with sharp, staccato barks.

"Flowers, Miss?"

The voice came from a side door she had not observed and Judy turned abruptly to see the familiar face of Sam Tucker, the florist. The place had been improved and remodeled since her last visit there, and now a door opened directly from the greenhouse into a wing of the yellow farmhouse next to it.

Judy stepped forward and held out her hand.

"Don't you know me any more, Mr. Tucker? I thought you and I were old friends."

"So we are. So we are," he agreed, giving her hand a hearty shake. "It's Judy Bolton sure enough this time. I should have known you right off, but the other day I made a fool blunder. Called out, 'Hello, Judy!' to some strange young woman who was driving through here with her folks. Close up, I could see it wasn't you, but I didn't want to make the same mistake again."

"That's funny," mused Judy. "I didn't think there was anyone else in the world who looked that much like me."

"I sure felt ashamed of myself," Sam Tucker admitted. "But young folks grow up and change so fast it's hard to keep track of 'em. You're Peter Dobbs, the young lawyer, aren't you?" he continued, turning to Peter. "I hear you're making out all right. The folks in Roulsville need a bright young fellow like you to help them out of their legal difficulties. But it's a long ride. I hear you drive in every day from Farringdon."

"It's not bad." Peter smiled at Judy. "Judy's my secretary," he explained, "and she rides with me. We're driving to Emporium this morning and that's twice as far."

The man chuckled and wagged his head.

"I see. I see," he murmured. "Young folks will be young folks. Bad roads and bad weather make no difference to them. But with the old ones it's different. It's been a hard winter for them, eh, Judy?"

She nodded, wondering if anyone had told him the sad news. But, somehow, she couldn't bring herself to say a word.

"Yep, it's been a hard winter," he went on. "Thought the cold weather'd let up come March. But it looks like winter's here for quite a spell yet. Used to be 'bout this time o' year that your Grandpa Smeed would come in to order his tomato plants. Fine tomatoes he raised from them, too. I recall how you used to tag along with him. You weren't more'n knee-high the first time your grandparents brought you in." He sighed deeply. "And now they're both gone. I s'pose you come in for flowers."

Judy told him that they had. She had been looking around while he was talking and had noticed a row of white carnations, as prim as paper flowers and just as lifeless. They wouldn't do, she decided. She wanted something more cheerful, something that would remind her of her grandparents alive and well as they had been at Christmas.

The Bolton family always spent their Thanksgivings and Christmases at the old homestead in Dry Brook Hollow. It was only a few miles above Roulsville and often Judy and Peter stopped there for supper on their way home from the office. But now? Would the house be empty? Or would Red Burnett, the hired man, stay on as caretaker? Who would tend the old-fashioned flower garden that used to be Grandmother Smeed's great pride? Hollyhocks, nasturtiums, snapdragons——''

"I know what kind of flowers we'll get," Judy spoke up, suddenly inspired, "the kind Grandma used to grow in her garden—a big spray of them. Could you make up a big spray of old-fashioned flowers and tie them with a ribbon?"

"Well, now, let's see," Sam Tucker began. "Snapdragons, lilies of the valley, cornflowers and maybe a little bunch of marguerites. You'd like some ferns?"

"Oh, yes! Like the ferns that grow in the woods around Grandma's place. It will always be Grandma's place," she told Peter later when they were in the car, "no matter who lives there. I suppose it will have to be sold," she finished sadly. "Grandma wouldn't have had time to make a will."

"That's where you don't know your Grandmother," Peter said. "You can depend upon it, she left everything in order. There was a will, too, although I never saw it. She drew it up in the proper legal form and Red told me he was witness to it. I think she meant to file it at the office, but then she had this sudden heart attack. I'm sure we'll find it somewhere in the house."

"I hope so. I'm not very eager to solve the mystery of a missing will," Judy told him. "In books they're always hidden in old clocks and secret drawers and I'm sure Grandma wouldn't do anything as foolish as that. She always kept her important papers in a drawer of her sewing machine."

"It will turn up in no time," Peter prophesied. "You can be thankful you haven't any scheming relatives to fight over the property as some of our clients have."

"I suppose I can," Judy agreed, "but do you realize, now that Grandma and Grandpa are dead, I haven't any relatives at all? There's only Dad and Mother and Horace and me. Of course, there's Miss Leonard," she added as they came into the outskirts of Emporium, "but she's only a make-believe aunt, as I told you. No real relative of mine ever had such a beautiful voice."

"Your voice isn't half bad," said Peter. "I like to hear you talk."

"It's easier not to think when you're talking. Here's the address Mother gave me," said Judy, reading it from a slip of paper.

Peter had some difficulty finding the house, but finally located it at the end of a hilly street. Several teachers boarded there and Judy and Peter were introduced to two of them. They discussed music while they were waiting for Miss Leonard. It was quite evident that the other teachers believed her to be the finest music teacher the Emporium school had ever had.

Miss Leonard was soon ready, looking almost as young as Judy in her fur jacket and fashionable little hat. She was still beautiful, but there was a sad expression in her eyes. It had been there ever since Judy could remember.

The sky had darkened in the few minutes they had spent inside the house and now a fine rain was falling. Every little twig and branch on the trees that nearly met over the narrow street had a thin frosting of ice. Judy could feel the car wheels slipping under them.

"I won't risk driving back without chains," Peter announced when they were at the foot of the hill. He parked near the business center of the town and, stopping only for a hurried lunch with Miss Leonard and Judy, proceeded to put them on.

"Let's do a little shopping at the department store while we're waiting for Peter," Judy suggested to Miss Leonard. "I wanted to get a black bag as my old red one is hardly suitable to carry into church. Patent leather is nice, now that

spring's coming, don't you think? And I do like
a bag with a zipper compartment and a change
purse that's attached so it can't be lost.''

Miss Leonard nodded understandingly. "I
know exactly the kind you mean. I'm particular
about my pocketbooks, too.''

They went directly to the leather goods counter
where there was a large selection of bags. Judy
had looked at only a few of them when a strange
man rushed into the store and hailed her with,
"Oh, there you are! You forgot your pocketbook.'' And, before Judy could protest, a shiny
black patent leather bag was thrust into her hand.

"But this isn't mine! You've made a mistake——''

The jangle of the store bell, ringing at one
o'clock, drowned out Judy's voice. The man who
had given her the bag had already disappeared
through the revolving door and left it swinging
so fast that it was a moment before she could
follow him.

"Wait a minute!'' she called, running after
some stranger who turned out to be the wrong man
after all.

There was nothing to do but return to the counter where Miss Leonard was waiting, looking as
bewildered as Judy felt. The saleswoman was
busy with another customer.

"I'll be with you in a minute,'' she said. "You
know, this is really my lunch hour.''

"But this bag isn't mine," Judy began.

"Well, it isn't mine, either," the clerk returned ungraciously. And, when she had finished with her customer, she deliberately walked away from the counter.

Judy was left holding her own shabby red purse in one hand and the shiny new black patent leather pocketbook in the other.

"What am I to do?" she asked helplessly. "I can't keep it."

"You can't very well give it back," Miss Leonard answered reasonably enough.

Just then Peter tooted his horn outside, urging them to hurry. There was no way out of it. Judy, feeling as guilty as though she had stolen the pocketbook, followed Miss Leonard back to the car.

CHAPTER II

"Well, did you get your bag?" Peter greeted them.

"I got a bag," Judy told him, "but I didn't exactly buy it. Somebody rushed into the store and handed it to me and then rushed off before I had a chance to give it back."

"Sounds as though the store was doing a rushing business," Peter commented.

"But seriously," she objected, "that's exactly the way it happened."

"Indeed it is," Miss Leonard put in. "I never saw a man in such a hurry. Naturally, Judy tried to follow him."

"Naturally," said Peter, "and I suppose he vanished before her eyes. I knew it was about time she ran into another ghost."

"It wasn't as bad as that," Judy assured him. "He didn't exactly vanish. He only darted into a revolving door and set it spinning. My head's spinning, too, I can tell you. Here I am with somebody else's bag and there isn't even time to look for the owner——"

"You're right there," Peter agreed. "We

11

mustn't lose another minute if we expect to be back in Roulsville for the services at two o'clock. They're to be held in the brick church," he added for Miss Leonard's information. "Now suppose you two pile in back and examine the contents of the bag and let me attend strictly to driving."

"That suits us," Judy agreed as she settled herself comfortably beside the music teacher. She pulled a robe over their laps, for it was growing colder by the minute. Then, eagerly, she opened the bag.

Miss Leonard tried not to show her curiosity.

"Maybe there's an address or something inside —" she began. But Judy interrupted excitedly: "Oh, good! Here's a letter."

To her great disappointment, the envelope was blank. There was nothing else inside the pocket-book—no zipper compartment, no change purse, nothing at all except the envelope. Judy hesitated a moment and then slit it open. Inside was a piece of plain paper on which it said in uneven printed letters:

I HAVE SOME INFORMATION WHICH MAY BE WORTH A FORTUNE TO YOU. SEE ME NEXT TUES-DAY AFTER THE LECTURE AND HAVE FIVE HUN-DRED DOLLARS IN SMALL BILLS. YOU WON'T BE SORRY.

Then followed a picture of a gun and the signature, *Blackie.*

Judy's eyes widened. It looked suspiciously like blackmail.

"It's probably a joke of some kind," Miss Leonard told her. "Young people are always making up codes between themselves and pretending to talk like big gangsters. I find plenty of such notes around the school. You can see that the gun is printed with a child's stamping set."

"But it wasn't a child who gave me the pocketbook. It was a man and I noticed that he was pretty careful not to show his face. What do you think of it, Peter?" Judy asked, after she had read the note aloud.

He gave a low whistle of surprise.

"Whew! You're headed for trouble, Judy. The quicker we get this information in the hands of the federal authorities, the better it will be for you."

"I see what you mean," she acknowledged. "I'd never let anyone sell me information. And I'm willing to bet something precious that this fellow, Blackie, is wanted by Uncle Sam's G-men. But what do we do about that?"

"I guess we'd better call up Washington. Golly! Who would have thought we'd ever run into a mess like this—and on a day like this."

"Couldn't you just forget it?" Miss Leonard asked in a weak voice.

"I could," Peter replied, "but I wouldn't. And here's why. Only last week I received a pamphlet from the government asking the aid of the legal profession in their fight against crime. They mentioned several rackets that they are trying to smash and blackmailing is one of them. Naturally, Judy and I want to help and, believe me, I'm thankful this pocketbook fell into our hands. We wouldn't have blackmailers if people weren't afraid.''

''I'm one of the timid souls, I guess,'' Miss Leonard admitted. ''I've lived so much in my music. But surely you're not going to bother the federal authorities with a little note you know nothing about.''

''Little notes sometimes cause big headaches,'' Peter said grimly, his eyes on the road.

''I'll call Washington if you want me to,'' Judy offered. ''It will be sort of thrilling saying, 'This is Judy Bolton, secretary to Peter Dobbs, the lawyer——''

''Goose! They won't know Peter Dobbs from Adam.''

''They will if we help the G-men. First thing, you know, you'll be running for district attorney and then, who knows, you may be president——''

''As if we hadn't enough troubles already,'' said Peter, glancing at his watch as they came in sight of the brick church in Roulsville. ''Well, it's just a quarter to two. We made it with fifteen minutes left over to call up Washington.''

''Perhaps you'd better do it, after all,'' Judy

suggested. "I'm supposed to join the family in the church parlor."

"Think you can find it?"

"Of course. It's right next to the minister's study. You go in this way." And she indicated an entrance around at the side.

"I'll come in quietly as soon as I've made the call."

"And I'll see about the music," Miss Leonard promised as they entered the small side door which opened into an anteroom with a stairway winding upward to the choir loft. Soon Judy could hear the music teacher's footsteps almost over her head.

She was not familiar with the church her grandparents had attended. She stood where Miss Leonard had left her, confronted by a number of closed doors with no indication of what might be behind them. One was the minister's study; one was the church parlor. But how was she to tell which one to open? And where did the other two doors lead?

"I'll try this one," she decided and was about to open it when a curious sound came to her ears. Did she imagine it or was somebody actually knocking on the other side of the door?

Knock! Knock! Knock! Judy heard it quite clearly now. She hesitated only a moment longer and then threw open the door. To her dismay, she found herself almost laughing at what she saw. Her brother Horace, the newspaper reporter who should have been able to squeeze in and out of all sorts of difficult places, had managed to lock himself in this particular room.

"Well, how did I know which door to open?" Horace sputtered, his face red with embarrassment. "I walk in here and open a door and *bam!* There I am headfirst in the baptismal pool. Lucky thing for me there was no water in it. As it was, I might have cracked my skull. I couldn't even call for help with the funeral just beginning outside. Now, Sis," he went on, his voice becoming persuasive, "you won't tell the folks what happened, will you? It's hardly appropriate to make a joke of it. I just came in quietly with you."

"Smooth your hair then. Here." She handed him a mirror and realized that she must look as queer as he did, carrying two pocketbooks. She explained briefly that she had found one of them. "I'll tell you all about it later," she promised. "In the meantime I think I'll leave my own pocketbook in here and come back for it afterwards."

"I should think you'd leave the pocketbook that you found. You might need your own."

Judy clutched the black patent leather bag still more tightly.

"I can't leave this pocketbook out of my hands for a minute!" she exclaimed in dismay. "I ran into something as surprising as you did and Peter's gone to call up the federal authorities in Washington. But I can't explain it all now. We must go into church."

"Miss Leonard got here all right, didn't she?"
Horace asked anxiously. "It isn't anything about
her, is it? Mother was so worried."

"Yes. She's here. Nobody's been kidnapped, if
that's what you're afraid of. It was just that we
wanted Washington to know what was in a letter
we found inside the pocketbook."

"Oh," said Horace, just as though it were un-
important.

Judy sighed at his lack of imagination and then
turned the knob of one of the other doors. To her
relief, it opened into the church parlor. The solemn faces of her parents and the hush that filled
the room reminded Judy again that she was at a
funeral, although it still seemed, unaccountably,
that both her grandparents were still alive back in
the dear old house in Dry Brook Hollow.

Now the music of the pipe organ filled the
church. An usher in black escorted the family to
their places and they listened in silence as the simple services were read. Peter had come in alone,
as he had promised, and was seated in one of the
back pews. He didn't look one bit as though he
had just finished making a thrilling telephone call
to Washington.

The prayer at the end of the service was followed by the sweet strains of the old hymn, *Lead
Kindly Light*. It seemed to come from far off
somewhere. The organist had played nearly all

the way through it before Judy realized that Miss Leonard wasn't singing. She was standing there in the choir loft exactly as though she meant to sing and people were glancing at each other, wondering. Judy touched her father's hand.

"Dad," she whispered, "what's the matter? Why isn't she singing?"

He shook his head and she knew she must not speak until after they were outside the church. But she could guess what had happened. Miss Leonard had lost her voice. Would she ever be able to sing again?

CHAPTER III

A Mysterious Ailment

Judy sat beside her father in the family car. They were on their way home, both of them quiet and thoughtful. Occasionally Judy would glance back to see if Peter's car was in sight. He would be driving home with his sister Honey and their grandparents who had come in spite of old age and bad weather. Dr. Bolton had brought them but now the back of his car was filled with flowers and potted plants to be distributed among his patients.

"Your grandmother always said flowers were meant for the living," the doctor remarked. "That's why your mother and I decided to give all her flowers away. One of the nicest plants goes to Grandpa and Grandma Dobbs and we've persuaded Miss Leonard to accept a beautiful potted lily."

"That's nice," Judy answered. "But, Dad, isn't there anything else we can do for her? I was just thinking that, without her music, Miss Leonard will be like a patient without medicine. I believe there's a quotation somewhere about music being the medicine of the breaking heart. Isn't it too bad she just grieved over Uncle John instead

of perking up again and taking an interest in someone else?''

Dr. Bolton gave a short laugh. "That's the way
modern girls do, isn't it? But I'm afraid Miss
Leonard isn't very modern. Instead of turning
to another romance, she found comfort in her
music. In her day a girl loved only once. She
didn't toss her heart back and forth from one boy
to another trying to decide.''

"Well, I've decided now," Judy returned. She
knew her father was referring to her own indeci-
sion. For a time she hadn't been able to make up
her mind whether it was Peter Dobbs or Arthur
Farringdon-Pett, the rich young architect, that
she wanted to marry. Her parents considered her
too young to be thinking seriously of marriage and
did not altogether approve of the diamond she now
wore on her finger.

Miss Leonard wore a diamond, too, the one
Judy's uncle had given her the day he enlisted in
the army. She was only sixteen then, a radiant
young girl with a voice like a lark. She was still
beautiful at thirty-eight. Judy could hardly believe that twenty years separated them; that Miss
Leonard was nearly as old as her mother. She was
exactly the same age Judy's Aunt Lucy would
have been if she had lived, and the two had been
chums, just as Judy and Honey were.

"I wonder if I'd be like that if anything happened to Peter," Judy said out loud.

"Like what, Judy girl?"

"Like Miss Leonard," she answered. "She looked so pathetic when she left the church with Mother, as if she hadn't a thing to live for. Mother was crying too."

"I know," Dr. Bolton said, "but there's still hope that this is only a temporary upset and will right itself by morning. Miss Leonard is staying with us tonight and I'm sure you'll do what you can to cheer her up."

"Of course, Dad, but if she still can't sing——"

"It hardly seems possible," the doctor answered. "Her speaking voice is as clear as ever. But naturally I intend to give that throat of hers a thorough going-over."

Judy swallowed hard. She knew, from her own experience, that her father's throat examinations could be most thorough.

"And then?" she questioned.

"Another interest," he declared. "Something that will make her forget this worry about her voice."

"Oh, Dad!" Judy exclaimed. "I know what. I could get her to help me solve my mystery."

"What, another one? I should think that baby mix-up in New York would have cured you."

"Nothing can ever cure me of wanting to find out things," she declared, "and right now I want to find out who owns this pocketbook."

The doctor looked at it in surprise.

"Isn't it yours?" he asked. "Then how do you happen to be carrying it?"

"I had to," she told him. "Someone gave it to me and then ran off before I could give it back. At first I thought it was only a mistake. I still think it's a mistake. But, Dad," she went on more anxiously, "there was a suspicious note in it and Peter thought it best to notify the federal authorities."

Dr. Bolton looked grave. "Perhaps you'd better let me see that note, Judy girl."

She unfolded it and read it aloud.

"I confess, I don't understand it," he admitted at last, "but it has all the earmarks of a puzzling mystery. I suppose you'll go about solving it in your usual whirlwind manner, in spite of the fact that it may be dangerous."

"Whirlwind is right," agreed Judy, thinking of the man in the department store. "But I do promise to be careful." She paused thoughtfully. "I wonder what they said in Washington."

"You'll soon know. Here we are at home," Dr. Bolton announced, stopping his car before the gate. It opened upon a wide lawn surrounded by a neatly trimmed hedge. The walk went straight to the door of the house and here Judy and her father parted, for he had a professional call to make.

Horace had already arrived with Miss Leonard and his mother. They had come in the minister's car and the good man was still there. All four of them were sitting around the living room fireplace. They looked as pale as ghosts in the flickering light. Blackberry, Judy's cat, was purring about their feet and a grotesque shadow of him was thrown on the opposite wall. He came forward to meet his mistress, as sedate as only a cat can be, and she bent to stroke him.

"We were discussing religion, dear. Come in and join us," Mrs. Bolton said.

Judy found a place on the sofa beside Miss Leonard and squeezed her hand in wordless sympathy as the discussion continued. The minister's words did not penetrate her mind until she heard the name, Peter. She started up and then sat down again in confusion as she realized he was reading from a book in the Bible called *Peter*. He was in the middle of something about an inheritance that fadeth not away being reserved in heaven for the righteous, when the telephone rang. Judy excused herself and answered it from an extension in the hall.

"Hello. Hello, Peter," she said eagerly. "I was waiting for you to call. Did you get the government offices all right? What did they say?"

"They're sending an agent around tomorrow. Can you be at the office?"

"What time?" she asked.

"They didn't say."

"I'll be in as soon as I can," she promised, "but you hadn't better wait for me. Miss Leonard and the minister are both here and Mother may need me in the morning. I'll tell you all about it when I see you.''

''What are you doing about that pocketbook?'' he asked. ''We may have to turn it over to the authorities, you know.''

''That's okay with me,'' she told him. ''I'll bring it along when I come to the office. Let's hope the agent doesn't arrive before I do. Peter,'' she asked eagerly, ''will he be a *real* G-man? I've heard so much about them.''

''I hope he will be. Take care of yourself, Angel.''

''I will,'' she promised. '' 'Bye, Peter. See you in the morning.'' And she hung up to find Horace at her elbow. Her brother's eyes had that cat-eat-mouse expression that meant he scented news.

''You haven't given me the dope on this,'' he charged, ''and I haven't a thing to hand in to the paper tomorrow.''

''News hound!'' Judy scolded. ''Well, this isn't for publication and, unless you promise not to write it up, I won't tell you a blessed thing.''

''Aw, Judy—'' he began.

''There's a reason,'' she assured him. ''Publicity may be dangerous. I may be in trouble this very minute. You see, there was a threatening note inside this pocketbook and, if I don't show up at a lecture—but don't ask me what lecture!—

well, something may happen. That's all. We are
going to try and keep it from happening, if we can,
and that's where Uncle Sam's G-men come into
the story.''

"But, Judy," protested Horace, "that's news.
The best the paper's had in weeks. Tell me how
you got hold of the pocketbook.''

"It was nothing," Judy replied, with a sweep of
her arms. "It fell into my hands like manna from
heaven. There are some people who walk into department stores and buy things and there are
others who walk in and have things given to them.
There are purse snatchers and purse giver-
outers——"

"But, Judy, that's good! That's humorous!
That'll make the front page!''

"I said," Judy informed him coldly, "that you
weren't to put it in. Do you want this crook to
know the G-men are after him? Do you want to
spoil our chances of helping them? I'm warning
you, if you do put anything in the paper about
this I, personally, shall stop in at the office and
give them another good story to appear right beside it, HERALD REPORTER TRAPPED IN BAPTISMAL
POOL, and, believe me, that's humorous too!''

"Judy, you wouldn't!''

"I certainly would if you haven't sense enough
to leave out this other story until this crook,
Blackie, is captured. But," she added after allowing him to read the note, "if you really want some-

thing to do you might help me find out what lecture he's talking about. Not that I intend to buy his information but, Horace, if we could help trap him, that would be news!''

''You're right, it would be. I see your point, Sis,'' he acknowledged, ''and I'll look up all the lectures in the neighborhood, if you think that will help.''

''It certainly won't do any harm,'' Judy assured him as they returned to the living room.

The minister was just leaving and Judy thought she heard Miss Leonard sigh as though she were a little tired of being comforted.

''We'll all feel better after the strain of this day is over,'' Judy told her that evening as she showed her to the guest room opposite her own. She brought clean towels and one of her own nightgowns which she said she hoped would fit.

''You're all so thoughtful,'' Miss Leonard remarked sadly. ''It isn't right when I spoiled the whole service——''

''But you didn't,'' Judy objected. ''The organ music was lovely by itself. You just feel badly about Grandma, I guess. I do, too, but Mother says we should be thankful that she and Grandpa went close together and didn't have to suffer or be lonely. I get choked up, just the way you did, when I think about it. But old people have to die and we have to bear it.''

''You dear girl, of course we do,'' the music

teacher agreed warmly. "I hope you're right and I was only choked up. Young people nowadays take things much more philosophically than we do. Everything is an adventure."

"You can join me in some of my adventures if you like, Miss Leonard."

She sighed, looking a little wistful, then said, "I wish you'd call me Linda."

It was rather pathetic, as though she were trying to recapture her youth as well as her music. Judy left her, positive that she wouldn't sleep a wink for worrying. But she was exhausted and fell asleep almost the moment her head touched the pillow. Her mother had to shake her the next morning to awaken her.

"We've all had breakfast," she announced, "that is, all but Miss Leonard. She didn't want any, and no wonder! Your father had just finished examining her throat. He found it in perfect condition, nothing at all wrong with her vocal cords and every evidence that she is well. So I ran over that hymn on the piano to see if she could sing it. But, Judy, it's the saddest thing. She opened her mouth and you could see she was trying, but still she couldn't sing a note. Your father doesn't know what to think and, to tell you the truth, he's afraid he can't do a thing for her."

"But, Mother," Judy exclaimed, "she's a music teacher! She can't go back to her school unless she can sing."

"We realize that, dear," Mrs. Bolton said. "We've persuaded her to stay here with us for a few days. A rest cure, we said. Your father says you have some plan that may help."

Judy considered this, hurrying into her clothes.

"I don't know what exactly. Today I simply must go to the office."

"I know," her mother answered. "Horace is taking you in that little runabout he always used to keep at Grandma's. He convinced me it was important."

"It certainly is," said Judy who was now dressed and ready. "I'm going to meet a G-man and find out what he thinks of the evidence we found in that black patent leather pocketbook."

CHAPTER IV

ARRIVAL OF THE G-MAN

JUDY burst into the office at eleven o'clock and, before Peter had a chance to say good morning to her, asked breathlessly, "Has he come yet?" And then, as the young lawyer shook his head, she handed him the pocketbook for safekeeping.

"Carrying this thing is like carrying a bomb," she declared. "I'm afraid somebody will point a gun at me and demand five hundred dollars at any minute. People have been killed for less than that."

Peter merely grinned, knowing Judy for the fearless girl she really was. She hung her coat and hat on the rack in the corner and went directly to her desk where several letters were waiting to be sorted over and answered. A long contract form also waited to be typed, but this routine work only made the adventurous part of the day more exciting. It would be nice, she thought, to have something very legal-looking in her typewriter when the G-man came in. The contract, between an employer and an employee of the Roulsville Light and Power Company, looked legal if not interesting and Judy immediately went to work on it.

29

Halfway down the first page she sighed and looked up at Peter.

"You don't suppose he'll mistake this office for a garage, do you?" she asked.

Peter guffawed.

"It's hardly bigger than one. You seem rather anxious to impress this F. B. I. man. What's the idea?"

"I don't know. Just silly, I guess," Judy answered and continued banging away on the typewriter keys.

A slick-haired client came in about noon, wanting information on wills and, at a nod from Peter, Judy took down a record of the conversation in her shorthand notebook. The man left his name and address, slapped a five dollar bill down on the table saying, "That's for your time, Counselor," and then departed.

Judy observed the startled look on Peter's face and then laughed.

"That's an easy way to earn five dollars," she commented. "Usually they don't offer to pay for legal information. They think it grows on bushes. Do you think he intended to make a will?"

"The way I have him figured out," Peter said grimly, "he's interested in getting hold of some money, not in giving it away. I wish he'd kept his five dollars. It leaves me in a difficult position. I don't want to be a party to any swindle he's trying to work. Judy, suppose you check up on that name and address. Kelly is an Irish name and I'd swear he's no Irishman.''

While Judy was busy looking through the directory a knock was heard on the office door. She glanced at Peter who grinned and motioned for her to let the visitor in.

He was a well-built, athletic chap with keen blue eyes which seemed to take in every detail of the room and its occupants at a glance.

''I'm David Trent from the Federal Bureau of Investigation,'' he announced. ''Are you Miss Bolton, the girl who received the threatening letter?''

''I am,'' Judy replied, trying to keep her voice from sounding as excited as she felt. ''And this is Peter Dobbs, my employer. He's the one who telephoned Washington.''

''Let me congratulate you for acting as promptly as you have,'' Mr. Trent said, extending his hand to Peter. ''You both seem to have taken this very calmly and that is unusual under the circumstances. Most of the potential victims in this sort of racket become excited and accede to the extortioner's demands at once. That's why it's so difficult to get a conviction.''

''I understand that, Mr. Trent. But in our case it's different,'' Peter explained. ''My secretary is not easily frightened and, as a matter of fact, it would be quite impossible for her to accede to these demands even if she wished to. She wouldn't know how to get in touch with the extortioner.''

"You see,'' Judy put in, fearing that Peter hadn't made it quite clear, "the note says 'I have some information which may be worth a fortune to you. See me next Tuesday after the lecture and have five hundred dollars'— Well, you can see that's ridiculous. There isn't anything I want to know worth five hundred dollars, and if there was, I'd find it out for myself. Besides, I'm not going to any lecture—'' She paused. "Or am I? My brother said he'd find out about lectures and it might be a good idea to attend one just to see what happens.''

"There, you see how it is,'' the G-man pointed out. "These fellows figure that a woman is going to be curious. They work on the grab-bag principle, half the time without having any real information. You say this note was handed to you in a pocketbook?''

"I have it right here,'' Peter said, passing the black patent leather bag to him over the desk.

Peter and Judy both watched the agent attentively as he examined it, studying both the note and the pocketbook under a glass.

"They probably buy these bags in quantities,'' he concluded, "and use them as traps. What woman is going to refuse a brand-new pocketbook or fail to open it to see what's in it? Having gone that far, they figure she'll go farther. *Information* is an intriguing word. Nearly every family has some secret and these scoundrels capitalize on curiosity and fear.''

''But I'm not afraid,'' Judy protested. ''Everyone who knows anything about me knows I'm not afraid of things.''

''Ah, but you are curious! You can't deny that, Miss Bolton. I tell you I know how these extortioners work. They have their victims classified in two groups—the timid and the curious. The first group will pay hush money to keep their secrets from being told; the second group will buy information.''

''I'm not in either group then,'' Judy declared, becoming a little vexed at his superior manner. ''I'm in a third group—a group that calls up the federal government and reports the extortion letter as the law tells us to do. I would have called up myself only I received this note on the afternoon of my grandmother's funeral and—well, I had to be in church.''

''I see. That sheds still more light on the subject. Your grandmother had just died and so it was quite evident that you would be upset and easily frightened——''

''But I tell you I wasn't upset! I wasn't frightened——''

Judy's voice broke. This was too much. He didn't have to drag her whole family into it, did he? She turned her face away so that he couldn't see how close she was to tears. To think that anyone, even the meanest crook, would write such a letter because he knew there had been a death in the family! She couldn't believe such a thing was possible.

"Perhaps," Peter suggested quietly, "you'd better let me give you the rest of the information, Mr. Trent."

"Oh, no! I'll give it to him," Judy said, turning quickly about. All traces of tears had vanished from her face. "You couldn't describe the man, Peter. You didn't see him and, to tell you the truth, I only had a glimpse of his face. He had his hat pulled down. But he was youngish, about thirty-five I should say, and he was rather small and wiry. I think he was an inch or so shorter than I and had a moustache. It was one of these dinky ones that look like eyebrows——"

The G-man laughed and Judy immediately forgave him for almost making her cry.

"That's observation for you," he declared. "That's the best description we've had of Blackie yet."

"So he's been described to you before?" asked Peter in surprise.

"Only vaguely," replied Mr. Trent, "but we have his fingerprints and several notes similar to this one on file in Washington."

"Then you know his real name?"

"No, only his nickname, Blackie. That must be short for blackmail. You see," the agent explained, "we have a file of nicknames as well as real names and aliases. We also have the largest collection of fingerprints in the world and yet they can be checked with amazing rapidity. The F. B. I. is out to get its man and we'll get Blackie."

"You mean without letting us help?" Peter asked anxiously.

"What could you do? You've already helped by furnishing us with this pocketbook."

"We might have theories—something you could work on," Peter replied. "Suppose it was a mistake about the pocketbook? Suppose it wasn't intended for my secretary at all, but for someone who looks like her?"

The G-man grinned.

"I think, Mr. Dobbs, that you'd go a long way before you'd find another girl who looks like your secretary. I can assure you that she's an unusual type. Red hair, gray eyes, rather an inquisitive tilt to her nose and definitely attractive. Too bad she's engaged, isn't it?"

Judy's face burned. He certainly hadn't overlooked anything. But Peter only grinned and said, "It would be too bad, but it just happens that she's engaged to me."

"Congratulations!" boomed Mr. Trent. "You'll make a grand team. Now if anything new turns up, call the field office." He presented a card with his name and telephone number and then bowed and took his leave. Judy turned to Peter.

"He didn't think so much of your idea, did he?"
Peter shook his head.

"Well, I do!" Judy declared. "There really
might be another girl who looks like me. Remember Sam Tucker, the florist? Well, he made a mistake and called some other girl 'Judy.' So why
couldn't the man who handed me the pocketbook
have mistaken me for someone else?"

"It seems reasonable enough," Peter admitted.
"We'll have to find out more about that girl from
the florist himself. If we can prove that there
really is another girl who looks like you, Judy, Mr.
Trent may change his mind about our helping."

"He probably suspects there's something we
haven't told him," mused Judy. "He said himself that nearly every family had its secrets."

"There's probably a great deal of truth in
that," Peter said thoughtfully. "Our family had,
you know. Honey and I might never have known
we were brother and sister if it hadn't been for
you. And there's the Farringdon-Petts and Dale
and Irene in New York. They all have secrets that
we know about and who can say how much else
there is that we don't know? But let's forget it
now and get back to work. Did you find that
man's name and address?"

"What man's? Oh, Kelly's? No, I didn't, but
I'm still looking." And to make good her state-
ment, Judy began scanning the pages of the directory in search of the name she had been told to

investigate just before Mr. Trent came in. She took out a smaller street directory and her face grew anxious.

"It can't be his real name," she announced. "At any rate, it's not his real address. There isn't any such street or any such number. He must be a crook or he wouldn't be afraid to let us know who he is."

"Perhaps we'd better describe him to your G-man, Judy."

"Now, Peter, don't tease me," she retorted. "He wouldn't be interested in anyone who simply came in here inquiring about wills——"

"Speaking of wills," Peter interrupted, "what about hunting up that will of your grandmother's? Horace and Honey could meet us at Dry Brook Hollow and the four of us search for it together. Say tomorrow after office hours."

"What about taking Miss Leonard along?"

"Miss Leonard!" exclaimed Peter. "Say, Judy, I forgot to ask you. Whatever happened to her at the funeral?"

"She lost her voice," Judy explained. "Even Dad doesn't know how it happened. She's staying at our house and I've promised to help by interesting her in something besides music. Maybe her voice will gradually come back again if she stops worrying about it. It sounds just the same when she talks. Anyway, I told her she could join me in some of my adventures."

"This won't be much of an adventure," Peter prophesied. "We know exactly where to look for the will and, from what your grandmother said, I have a general idea of what's in it."

"Just the same," Judy declared, "it's going to be an adventure—opening Grandma's sewing machine drawers, looking at all her treasures. You know, Peter, we were never allowed to touch those things when we were children and it will be a little like doing something we shouldn't to touch them now."

Peter glanced up from his desk to where she stood uncertainly beside him.

"And you were the one," he remarked, "who doubted that every family had its secrets."

CHAPTER V

THE OLD HOUSE SPEAKS

THE house in Dry Brook Hollow was a little off the main-traveled highway between Roulsville and Farringdon, and, in the summer, the thick leaves of the trees in Grandma's grove hid it from view. But on the cold March day when Judy, Peter, Horace, Honey, and Linda Leonard approached it, the house could be clearly seen through the naked branches of the trees.

"How lonesome it looks!" was Judy's first thought, but she said nothing for fear of depressing the others.

Two front doors, side by side, opened onto a low front porch from which, Judy remembered, she had often swung herself over the back of Ginger, her grandfather's spirited horse. Ginger had once made a hero of Horace, carrying him back toward the threatened town of Roulsville with his frantic cry, "The dam is breaking!" Judy had heard the crash, later, when the dam actually did break, from this very porch.

When she was a very little girl Judy used to call the two doors "the Sunday door" and "the everyday door," for one opened into the great living

39

room of the old farmhouse and the other opened directly into the kitchen.

For some reason that she was unable to explain, even to herself, Judy now chose the Sunday door and rapped softly with her knuckles on the outside of the glass.

"Red won't hear that," Peter told her and began banging more loudly on the panels of the everyday door.

"Peter, don't!" begged his sister Honey, clutching his sleeve. "It doesn't seem right when—when——"

"That's so," agreed Horace quickly. "I've got a key and so it's not at all necessary to rap."

Saying this, he turned his key in the lock of the Sunday door and then, hesitating only a moment, pushed it open.

"Red!" he shouted loudly through the still house.

A hollow echo answered him and Honey moved closer to Miss Leonard and clutched her arm.

"I don't think I'm going to like going in there—" she began.

"There's really nothing to be afraid of," the music teacher assured her. "The house won't seem any different once we're inside."

"Of course it won't," Judy urged, pulling her by the hand.

Everything in the living room was exactly as Judy remembered it. Grandma's plants, all carefully tended and watered, lined the window sills.

The rag carpet that covered the floor was as bright and pretty as ever. And there, on the marble-topped table, were the same pencil boxes, magazines and paper weight. The paper weight had a flower inside the glass and Judy always used to wonder how it got there. She had asked her grandmother once and the old lady had said, "Now wouldn't that beat all what questions a child can think up to bother folks with?"

Judy had learned, very early, that her grandmother seldom explained things. "Figure it out for yourself," she would advise, or, "Look it up in the dictionary." Thus the fat green dictionary was well thumbed, as were most of the books that lined the shelves of the high mahogany bookcase. The pictures in the room were all familiar—a lion solemnly watching a sunrise, cows in a quiet pool, a procession of famous musicians over the piano, a single rose in a carved mahogany frame. Judy loved them all. On winter evenings she used to sit before the great stone fireplace at the far side of the living room and imagine stories about them.

Yes, everything was the same and yet, in spite of what Miss Leonard had said, the house did seem different. They could all feel it. It was almost as if they could hear the absence of the familiar voices that used to welcome them.

"Judy, turn on the radio," Miss Leonard whispered. "A little music might help. I can still enjoy it even if I can't sing."

So Judy turned the dials of the radio that she

and Horace had given their grandparents for Christmas. Luckily, she was able to tune in on soft concert music. It was neither too gay nor too mournful. It made the quiet room suddenly come to life.

"There, is that better?" she asked, turning away from the radio.

"Much better," Miss Leonard agreed. "We aren't intruding now."

But still Honey shivered. The house was chilly and Peter made a fire. The wood was ready in a basket beside the fireplace.

"Still better?" he inquired.

And now everybody agreed that the living room was quite cheerful. The wind moaned outside, to be sure, but you couldn't hear it with the fire crackling and the radio going.

"I wonder where Red is," Honey said, pausing at the door that led from the living room into the immense old kitchen.

"Down at the barn probably," was Horace's guess. It was just about chore time and there were cows to be milked, chickens, pigs and two horses to be fed. The cows were Jerseys and gave the creamiest milk anyone could possibly imagine. Grandma used to make butter which Grandpa peddled to a few choice customers in Roulsville before the flood that washed all the old homes away.

Roulsville was new now. It was a boom town as unlike the old Roulsville as Peter's tiny office was unlike this immense old farmhouse. The kitchen was one of the largest rooms in the house. The old couple had practically lived in it, for it really combined kitchen, dining room and sewing room. The big range was at the far end, a large dining table occupied the center of the room and in one corner was a dish closet which reached to the ceiling. It was filled with Grandma's best dishes, some of them priceless old pieces of Wedgwood that had been in the family for over a hundred years.

Judy loved this kitchen. It gave her a feeling of the permanence of things. But now that her grandmother was dead the thought came to her that the house might be sold to someone who would change it all around; someone who would put up partitions to close off the wide spaces or tear down that beautiful dish closet.

"Horace," she asked her brother, "if Grandma left this house to you, you wouldn't sell it, would you?"

"Gosh!" he said. "I don't know. I don't know what I'd do with it. Maybe she left it to Mom."

"But what would your mother do with it?" Miss Leonard inquired. "She couldn't live here when your father has built up his practice in Farringdon."

"Horace was always her favorite," Judy began.

"Nonsense!" Horace interrupted. "You were. She always scolded the people she liked best. Remember how she used to fuss at Grandpa and all the time it was just because she couldn't get along without him.''

"Poor Grandma! I guess she couldn't," Judy agreed, taking a step toward the sewing machine where she knew the will must be.

The drawers were elaborately carved with grinning gargoyles holding the drawer pulls in their teeth. These creatures had always fascinated Judy. She used to imagine that they would snap at anyone who attempted to open the drawers without her grandmother's express permission.

"Do they bite?" Peter asked as she hesitated, eyeing the gargoyles with suspicion.

"They might—if we did anything against Grandma's wishes. Horace, do you remember which drawer it was?"

"Top on the left, wasn't it?"

"I thought it was the bottom on the right."

The sewing machine had six drawers in all. Seven, counting the small one for needles and bobbins. It was a machine such as one seldom sees nowadays, the best of its kind in 1890 when it was new.

"Let's each take a drawer," Honey suggested. "There's one for each of us and one left over."

"We won't bother with the button drawer, then," Judy told her. "I know what's in it, anyway, because Grandma used to let us play with her buttons. We played they were soldiers and Horace and I had battles and scattered them all over the room. Some of them were beauties. See!''

And she pulled the button drawer open a little way so that the soldiers of long ago looked out from their hiding place.

''I thought you weren't going to bother with that drawer,'' Horace teased her.

''I'm not,'' she retorted, sliding it back in its place. ''We'll each take one of the others.''

''I'll take this one,'' Miss Leonard said, pulling the top left-hand drawer all the way out and emptying the contents into her lap.

''Soap coupons,'' Horace announced as he pulled out the drawer below it. ''I wonder what Grandma was saving them for.''

''And this,'' observed Peter as he took the bottom drawer, ''was where she kept her thread. That finishes the drawers on the left side. But how about those on the right?''

''We're looking,'' Judy answered, for she and Honey were already examining the contents of the last two drawers.

''Any luck?'' Miss Leonard asked after a moment. ''I found only a few odd bits of sewing and crochet work and a ball of twine in this one.''

''There are patterns in here. Such funny old-fashioned clothes!'' Honey exclaimed. ''These must be nearly as old as the sewing machine.''

''And mine,'' said Judy, ''seems to be filled with letters. But no, here is an address book. This must be the drawer! And here is the deed to the wood lot across the road and here, oh my goodness! Grandma couldn't have put this here!''

"What?" asked Peter, coming closer to see. "As I live and breathe, it's a deck of playing cards!''

"Shocking!" exclaimed Miss Leonard. "You know how your grandmother felt about playing cards, Judy. She wouldn't allow a deck to be seen in her house——''

And at that moment, as if protesting against such a sacrilege, the house itself began to creak and groan. The cards, apparently without anyone having touched them, spilled off the edge of the sewing machine and slithered down over the noses of the gargoyles. Judy half expected the gargoyles, too, to come to life and, when a moment later a great crash sounded from somewhere, she glanced at them first and then at Peter.

"What's that? Oh, my goodness! What's *that?*''

Honey took a quick step backwards into the thread drawer which no one had thought to replace. It tipped, sending the many-colored spools of thread rolling in every direction while the others tripped over them in their hurry to reach the door.

The crash sounded again, even louder than before. Judy called from the living room. "It's upstairs! Come on, everybody! I'm going up there and find out what's happened.''

CHAPTER VI

A Plaster Ghost

Peter paused long enough to turn off the radio, for the concert was over and a man was now lecturing on accidents in the home. While it may have been appropriate, for no one yet knew what had happened, they were hardly in the mood to hear it. The welcome silence was broken by the sound of footsteps over their heads.

"I knew it!" Judy declared. "Someone's been touching Grandma's things. Those playing cards were deliberately left in the sewing machine drawer and goodness knows what's been taken!"

"But, Judy," Horace protested, "that wouldn't be your burglar upstairs."

"How do you know who it would be?" she retorted. "The only way to find out is to go up and see. Then, whoever it is, he'll have to answer to us."

Judy sounded very brave. She was about to turn the knob of the stair door when she heard footsteps—*thump! thump! thump!*—descending the stairs.

"Who's there?" demanded Peter, throwing open the door and standing back aghast as a cloud of white dust billowed out into the room. Behind the cloud came a man whom Judy recognized after her first moment of stunned surprise.

"Red!" she gasped. "What's happened? You're as white as a ghost. Your suit and everything is covered with it. Where have you been?"

"Asleep," Red admitted, "until this earthquake, or whatever it was, woke me up. Don't ask me what's happened. Come up and see for yourselves."

"It's plaster dust," Peter announced as he gained the head of the stairs. "There's been a weak place in the plaster and this wind has broken it loose."

"It's in my room!" cried Judy. "Look!" She pointed to the ceiling of the little bedroom her grandmother had always called hers and, sure enough, a great piece of plaster had fallen from it, striking the foot of the bed where it broke and scattered in every direction.

"Isn't it lucky no one was sleeping there—" Horace was about to say. But Red interrupted him.

"Lucky nothing! *I* was sleeping there. And if you think a sandstorm in the Sahara is something, you just ought to be around when it rains plaster. I can tell you it's no picnic." He paused, shook the house with a thunderous sneeze, and then sputtered, "It's even in my eyelashes!"

Honey giggled at that.

"You look like Santa Claus, minus the beard."

"But, Red," Judy questioned, "why were you sleeping in my room? That wasn't the room you used to have when Grandma was alive."

"Change of scenery," he answered sheepishly. "I was all in. Up late last night and had to catch up on my sleep. Golly! It must be chore time."

"It's past chore time," Horace told him with an attempt at severity. The attempt was spoiled by the helpless look he gave Judy. Who was Red's boss now, his eyes seemed to ask.

She shook her head.

"Maybe you'd better help him with the chores," she suggested to her brother.

"That's all right. You don't need to bother. But," the hired man added, "if you want to help clean up this mess it's okay with me. I ain't much of a hand with a dust rag."

It was evident that someone had to clean up. Someone had to see about repairing the house as well. Judy felt suddenly as though she wanted to cry. Everything was going to pieces. Her lovely little room with the sprigged wallpaper and the delightful old-fashioned paintings was now heaped with broken plaster. One of the pictures had fallen off the wall and the frame was broken. Miss Leonard bent and picked up the winsome little lady with a daisy chain in her hand.

"This was Lucy's favorite picture," she said sadly. "What a shame that it had to be broken! Judy, would you mind if I kept it and had it reframed?"

"Would I mind? It isn't mine," she answered uncertainly.

"But, Judy, your grandmother said you were to have the things in this room," Red told her. "There's a whole chest full of things she meant for you. The keys are in her sewing machine drawer."

"Judy!" Honey exclaimed, remembering. "We left all the drawers out of the sewing machine and the spools all over the floor. I'll run down and clean up."

"Do," Judy urged, "and bring the keys."

"They're in the small drawer in the top," Red called as she started down the stairs.

"We didn't look there," Miss Leonard suddenly remembered.

"I figured you were looking for something," Red said. "What was it?"

"Grandma's will," Judy answered. "Did she tell you where she put it?"

"She didn't need to," Red declared. "I put it in the sewing machine drawer myself. It was in the bottom one on the left-hand side along with her other papers."

"That was the drawer with the playing cards in it," Peter put in with a meaning glance toward Red.

"Playing cards? Who said so?"

"We found them," Horace declared. "I don't suppose you would have any idea how they got there."

"Well, now I might," Red admitted, wiping his face with his handkerchief. "I wouldn't swear to it, mind you. But one of my pals may have put them there. We had a little game last night and there was an argument about some of the cards being marked. Well, the marked deck couldn't be found when my pals were ready to go home."

"And who were your pals?" Judy demanded. "And how did you happen to be playing cards in my grandmother's house the day after her funeral? Haven't you any respect for her wishes at all, Red? You've had a good home here and a good job and a chance to do a little landscape gardening on your own. Grandma's treated you almost like a son. I really would have thought you might have shown some consideration——"

"Aw heck! I know all that," Red admitted, hanging his head. "Not that I'm against a friendly game of cards now and again. But you're right. We shouldn't have played here. It wasn't my idea, mind you. The boys just came over and so what were we to do?"

"I don't know," Judy answered, now thoroughly disgusted. "Who were they? Where did you meet them? I want to know their names in case anything's happened to Grandma's will."

"Red's friends wouldn't have touched it," Peter put in. "Nobody outside of your family would be interested."

"That's right," Red agreed. "If anybody's touched it most likely it was the old lady herself.

She might have changed her mind about leaving it in the sewing machine drawer and put it in that chest of things she meant for you."

"Why, of course," Judy agreed. "That's probably exactly where she put it. Thanks, Red. I didn't mean to be so—so critical."

"That's all right," grinned Red, wiping his face with his handkerchief again as he went out.

Judy turned toward the chest which, like everything else in the room, was white with plaster dust. Horace had already procured a broom and was busily sweeping up the broken plaster.

"We can't clean a thing until this dust is settled," Miss Leonard remarked, "and it really wouldn't be wise to open the chest until it's dusted."

"No, I suppose not," Judy agreed, "but I am curious to see what's in it."

At that moment Honey returned with the keys. She had no difficulty in finding them, she said, but took time to search the sewing machine drawers a little more thoroughly and replace all the spools of thread.

"And I'm sure the will isn't there," she added. "Someone must have taken it."

"Red says Grandma may have put it in my chest," Judy told her, "but we have to clean up the room before we look."

"That will make us hurry all the faster," Honey returned, seizing a dustcloth and beginning to rub vigorously on the rungs of a chair. But no sooner had she cleaned a place than the dust settled on it again, leaving it nearly as white as before.

Peter threw open all the windows, remarking, "Maybe that will clean the air."

The wind rushed through the room, picking up the picture Miss Leonard had saved from the broken frame and nearly blowing it away. Luckily, she caught it just in time.

"Maybe the wind is the thief who took the will," Horace observed, turning toward the stairs with his dustpan full of plaster.

"It isn't likely Grandma would leave it around where the wind could blow it away. Besides," Judy added, "people don't open their windows this wide except—except——"

She stopped, sneezing almost as loudly as Red had done.

"Let's go downstairs till the room's aired a little," Miss Leonard suggested. "You're catching cold."

"It's only the plaster," Judy insisted. "The wind is making it worse."

"Why not get away from it then?" asked Horace. "How about taking the chest down with us and opening it in the living room?"

"Perhaps Judy would rather open it by herself—" Peter began.

"Oh, no!" Judy interrupted. "I think it's a grand idea to open it downstairs by the fire. Will you take one end, Peter?"

"And I'll take the other," Horace offered.

When the two boys had lifted the chest, they found it to be very much lighter than either of them had expected it to be.

"There's no gold in it; that's certain," joked Peter.

"Must be filled with feathers," Horace remarked as they started down the stairs, each holding one of the handles.

The others followed. Judy's eyes were shining with anticipation.

"Don't you just love opening old chests?" Honey asked her.

"I'm sure your grandmother left you something beautiful," Miss Leonard said as she tucked her arm into Judy's.

"I'm sure she did, Linda," Judy replied warmly. "I promised you an adventure, didn't I? Then how would you like to turn the key in the lock and open the chest?"

"But it's your chest——"

"I know it," Judy said, "but it's your adventure. You'll do it, won't you—to please me?"

And Miss Leonard, smiling, nodded. She was ready to open the chest.

CHAPTER VII

SEARCHING FOR THE WILL

IN THE living room the fire had burned low, leaving only a bed of bright coals which had formed into curious shapes that looked almost like toy castles aflame. Horace poked them apart and threw on another log.

"There you are, Judy," he said, "just as cozy and warm as though you were right at home."

"Why, Horace! I am at home," she replied. "No house will ever come nearer being my home than this one. Think of all the summers we've spent here—all the times we've been sick and Grandma's taken care of us. Think of the times you've helped Grandpa in the fields——"

"And the time you almost got killed breaking in his colt," added Horace as they all gathered around the chest.

Judy handed Miss Leonard the key.

"I feel like Pandora opening her box," she said as she turned it in the lock.

"Oh, no," objected Honey, "you must have forgotten. Pandora's box was filled with—with diseases," she added, alarmed at what she was saying. Miss Leonard must have been worrying again about whether or not she would ever be able to sing.

"Well, there was Hope at the bottom," Judy put in brightly. "I wonder what's at the bottom of this box. I wonder——"

"There!" announced the music teacher, throwing open the lid. "Now you don't need to wonder. You know!"

"Oh!" exclaimed Judy, delighted at what she saw. "All of Grandma's needle paintings!"

And she held up a piece of cloth on which was embroidered in beautiful pastel colors a heron fishing on a blue lake. Next came a garden with nodding flowers. Then followed a little thatched cottage beside a road, beautifully worked in embroidery. The needle paintings were finished and ready for framing. A note pinned to them read:

Judy, will you please see that Linda gets these. She always liked them. Grandma.

"They're yours," Judy announced, placing them in Miss Leonard's lap and showing her the note.

"But I thought the things in the chest were for you——"

"So did I," Judy said, "but I guess Red made a mistake. This one isn't for me either."

She was already taking out the next object, a bedspread crocheted by hand. It was marked for her mother. Beside it was the box of ivory chessmen which Grandpa Smeed always insisted were his one extravagance.

Judy, will you please give these to Horace, it said on the note attached.

"But, Judy——"

"Sh!" she cautioned. "Grandma knew that you would like them. You're the only one in the family who could beat Grandpa at chess, you know."

Horace was obliged to accept the box of chessmen, but still he looked puzzled as did all the others. Judy dove deeper and deeper into the chest, bringing forth article after article. Each coveted treasure was marked for someone else.

"Judy, there must be some mistake," Honey told her sympathetically. "It was your treasure chest."

"I thought it was, you mean. It's probably all explained in the will," Judy answered, "but it doesn't seem to be here."

Red came in, a pail of foamy milk in either hand.

"Well," he asked, pausing on his way to the spring house back of the kitchen, "did the will show up or didn't it?"

"Not yet," Judy replied, "but we haven't yet reached the bottom of the chest. When did Grandma mark these things? It must have taken her ages."

"Right after she made her will," Red replied.

"I thought the will would be on top. She made it all right. I was witness and she willed me that piece of ground where I've been growing shrubs. There's five acres of it and I can tell you I thought that was pretty swell."

Peter looked up in surprise. "But, Red, if you were a beneficiary under the will, you shouldn't have been a witness. The will isn't valid unless it can be proved without your signature."

"Gosh! I didn't know that," Red answered, "but two of my pals were there and they signed it too. Does that make it okay?"

"It makes it okay all right," Peter said, "*if* we can find the will."

"And if we don't find it?" asked Horace, who could see that Judy had nearly emptied the chest. "What happens then?"

"Legally, everything would go to your mother as the only living child of your grandmother. Grandchildren do not inherit when their parents are living," Peter told him.

"That wouldn't be so bad, would it, Sis?" Horace asked, turning to Judy. "I should think Mom ought to have everything, anyway."

"What about Red's piece of land? He's really earned that," Judy declared, "and the rest of Grandma's property certainly ought to be divided the way she wished it. What about these pals of yours who were witness to the will, Red? I suppose Grandma read it aloud so that you knew what was in it?"

"Nope, she said that wasn't necessary," Red explained. "I wouldn't have known about my own land if I hadn't just happened to glance up and see my name. It ain't really Red, you know. It's Robert."

Judy smiled. She hadn't been wondering about Red's name, only about the names of his pals.

"Exactly what was said?" Peter inquired. "The law requires certain forms, you know, to make the will regular."

"It looked regular all right to me," Red replied. "She called me into her room and said, real important-like, 'Red, this is my last will and testament. Will you and your friends please watch me sign it?' So me and my pals, Button and Blackie——"

"Blackie!" exclaimed Judy, her eyes wide with apprehension.

"Sure, he and Sid Button are a couple of guys I met last winter when I was trading down to Emporium. They've been right nice, too. Witnessed the will as nice as you please and then Blackie says, 'Come on, Red. I'll help you with the chores.' "

"That was real sweet of him, wasn't it" said Judy, her lips tightening. "He wouldn't be one of those pals you had in here playing cards last night?"

"Sure he was——"

"Then," said Judy with a sigh, "I can just imagine what happened to the will."

"Gosh! What have I done?" gasped Red, his face as blank and innocent as a child's.

"Don't blame him too much," Peter advised Judy. "Remember, your grandmother trusted these men too. Wouldn't it be better to let Red know who his pals are and ask him to help us?"

"I guess it would," Judy agreed and so she and Peter, interrupting each other and with an occasional word from Horace or Miss Leonard, told Red about the note signed "Blackie" and stamped with a gun. They also told him how Blackie himself had given Judy a pocketbook. She described him and Red agreed that the man who had darted through the revolving door, leaving the mysterious bag, was none other than his pal who had witnessed the will.

"Gosh!" he said. "And I don't even know his address. I'd sure like to help you find him."

"You know the address of this other fellow, Sid Button, don't you?" asked Peter.

"Oh, sure. He has a business in Emporium. Maybe we could trace Blackie through him."

"It begins to look as though we were finding out something," Judy observed. "We'll have to turn over all this information to Mr. Trent——"

"Who's Mr. Trent?" Red asked, curious.

"Just a G-man I know," Judy answered and smiled to see his mouth drop open in astonishment.

"A G-man? Good Lord! Then they're hunting Blackie for blackmail? Believe me, Judy, I will

help you. I haven't forgotten the time you and
Peter got me out of jail when those fur robbers
framed me.''

''And we haven't forgotten that you helped us
solve one of our biggest mysteries,'' she told him.

''You bet!'' Peter agreed. ''If you hadn't
helped us trace Lorraine Lee and that double
ring . . .''

He stopped. Judy's look stopped him. He had
almost told a secret that he and Judy were pledged
to keep. No one must ever know that the engagement ring Arthur Farringdon-Pett had placed on
Lorraine's finger had first been given to Judy.
She had kept the baby mix-up in New York a
secret, too. And now, as they talked, she began to
suspect that there were other people who kept
secrets as well as herself. Family secrets. Could
it be true that nearly every family had them?

Honey, who had been sitting silently beside the
chest all this time waiting for Judy to open the last
package in it, now spoke up.

''I'm afraid I don't see what all this talk about
Blackie has to do with your grandmother's will,''
she said. ''Why would Blackie take the will? If
the property all goes to your mother, how could it
possibly be of any advantage to him?''

''She's right. You see,'' Horace said proudly,
''even beautiful girls sometimes use the gray matter under their golden locks.''

''Meaning I'm not beautiful?'' said Judy, tilting

her nose and making a wry face at her brother.

"Don't mention her hair," warned Red. "I have my own ideas about red-heads."

"Pretty clever as a rule, aren't they? All joking aside," Peter continued, "there still remains a possibility that Blackie may have taken the will with the idea that some of us would pay to get it back. Perhaps he imagines you would, Red. That is, if he knows about your piece of property——"

"But he knows I'm broke. How could I pay?"

"How could any of us for that matter?" asked Horace. "If you ask me, no clever crook is going to try and pick such slim bones as we are. Isn't it more likely that the will was removed from the sewing machine drawer simply to make room for the cards that were placed there? As I remember it, that drawer was pretty full."

"Say, that's an idea!" Red exclaimed. "If the will doesn't show up at the bottom of that chest, I'll help you look."

"I'm afraid you'll have to help us then," Judy announced as she lifted the last article out of the chest revealing only the bare strips of cedar wood at the bottom.

"Okay," agreed Red picking up the two pails which had been standing near the door, "I'll be back as soon as I've taken care of this milk."

"Wait a minute!" Honey pleaded. "You haven't seen what's in this package. Hurry and open it, Judy. We're all curious."

"You can't be any more curious than I am," she answered. "You'd think a package as big as this would be heavy, wouldn't you? But it isn't. It's as light as a feather."

"Maybe it's a feather pillow," Miss Leonard suggested.

"Maybe," agreed Judy, snipping the string with scissors from her grandmother's workbasket. It was among the things she had taken out of the chest and was marked for her mother.

The package was carefully wrapped in pale blue tissue paper tied with tinsel string. No note was attached to it so Judy unwrapped it herself. The paper fell away and she discovered, not a feather pillow at all, but a beautiful patchwork quilt.

CHAPTER VIII

The Memory Quilt

"Grandma's necktie quilt!" exclaimed Horace, peering over his sister's shoulder. "She'd been making it ever since I can remember. See!" And he pointed out dozens of tiny pieces of paper which fluttered like flags from the quilt. "She's pinned a note on every piece to tell us what it is."

"How sweet of her to tag them all!" cried Judy, pressing the soft quilt against her face as though it were a kitten. One of the sharp pins pricked her a little, like a kitten's claw, but she only hugged the quilt closer. "This must be for me since all the others were for somebody else. Horace," she asked, "wouldn't you think it was for me?"

"Certainly, if you want it. It's only a quilt——"

"Only a quilt? How can you say that? It's a lifetime of memories. Look, everybody! Honey! Linda! Peter! Come closer and look," Judy beckoned them. "Just see all the work Grandma's put into this. And she's tagged every piece!"

"'There's your mother's wedding dress," Honey

said, pointing to the tag on one of the light pieces.

The quilt was made of dark and light pieces of cloth joined together so that the dark pieces looked like neckties with the light pieces as their background. It was a beautifully made quilt, every stitch carefully sewed by hand and the whole thing tied with fluffy knots of green yarn. But it wasn't the beauty of the quilt that made it such a treasure to Judy. It was because of the story that each separate piece of material had to tell.

"Here's my yellow and blue flowered dress, the one I wore to the spelling bee that night I won the prize. You bought the cloth and I made the dress myself. Remember it, Horace?" asked Judy.

"As if I could ever forget it!" he answered. "That was the last time we ever went to a party in Roulsville. The next day the dam broke——"

"But here's a pleasanter memory," Miss Leonard put in as Judy spread the quilt across her lap. "Horace's first suit. He wouldn't remember it. He was only two. But he called it his candy suit, because it was striped like a stick of candy."

"I declare! I do remember it. Or perhaps I only remember the piece. This black and white figured one was my z-waist. I'm sure I remember that," Horace said.

"What's this piece?" asked Honey, pointing to a delicate pink-figured square.

"*Lucy's first party dress,*" Judy read from the slip of paper attached.

"Who was Lucy?"

"My aunt that died. I had an uncle that died too—Uncle John. That left only Mother out of Grandma's whole family," Judy explained.

"These were their dresses and waists when they were children," Miss Leonard pointed out. "I remember them all. And here's one of mine," she added. "Your grandmother made it for my birthday. I was just sixteen. I wore it the first time I sang in the choir. I chose my own song and, would you believe it, I picked out that old hymn *Will There Be Any Stars in My Crown,* because my dress had stars in it. See them. Little white circles of stars on the pale blue cloth. I thought they were beautiful."

"They are," agreed Judy. "The whole quilt is beautiful. Grandma couldn't have given me anything that I would have liked better. That is, if she meant this quilt for me."

"Of course she did, Judy."

"Well, I'll let myself think so anyway," she said as she continued studying the notes which her grandmother had pinned so carefully to every piece.

"Here's another one of Lucy's dresses," observed Peter who was now studying the quilt as eagerly as all the others.

"I remember the night she wore it," Miss Leonard put in dreamily. "We went to a square dance in Roulsville and John brought us home. Lucy pouted all the way because she had no one but her brother for an escort. As if anyone could want a finer escort than John!''

''That was just before the war, wasn't it?''

The music teacher nodded, lost in a dream of the past.

''Here's one of your grandmother's own dresses, Judy. This gray print. I remember it,'' said Honey. ''It was not so long ago that she wore it.''

Judy turned to look at the piece and suddenly tears filled her eyes. She hadn't really cried for her grandmother but now she couldn't seem to stop. She had worn that dress so many times. She was always bustling around, too busy to talk, too filled with life and vigor to be bothered answering questions. And now all the questions Judy might have asked her would remain forever unanswered.

''If I had only known how short a time Grandma would be with us, if we could have had just one heart-to-heart talk——''

Miss Leonard shook her head sadly.

''She wouldn't have told you much, Judy. There were a great many things your grandmother thought it best to keep to herself. Not once, in all the years since his death, did she mention your Uncle John and as for Lucy—well, you'd hardly expect her to speak of Lucy.''

''Why not?'' asked Horace. ''Mother often speaks of her. Was it because she ran away?''

''Did she?'' asked Honey, becoming more and more interested.

"She eloped!" Judy announced dramatically. She spread the quilt a little wider and added, "Here's the square that tells the story."

The square Judy pointed out was a piece of yellow voile dotted with tiny brown butterflies and the note attached to it read, *Dress Lucy wore the day she ran away to be married.*

"Who did she marry?" questioned Horace. "I don't believe Mother ever told us."

"That," said Miss Leonard, "is something no one seems to remember. Your grandparents knew his name, of course. They went to his home a year later to attend Lucy's funeral, but I doubt if they were very cordial to her husband. They never did approve of him. He worked in a circus side show and you can well imagine how horrified they were when they discovered that Lucy was meeting him without their permission."

"And then she married him?"

"Yes. She eloped just as Judy told you but what happened after that we can only guess. Your grandparents always insisted that her husband was brutal, inhuman—oh, I can't say what all. And no doubt they had some reason for thinking so. Anyway, the poor girl was laid to rest when she was only twenty. You saw her grave right beside your grandmother's. They brought her home to be buried and that was more than they could do for John who was killed in France——"

"Linda," pleaded Judy, "must we talk about it?

Grandma wanted the quilt to remind us of pleasant things, I'm sure.''

''But Lucy was a gay little thing,'' Miss Leonard insisted. ''Gay and reckless and daring—a little like you would be, Judy, if your parents didn't give you so much freedom. Perhaps rebellious is the word. I always thought this dress with its butterfly pattern just suited her. She was forever looking on the bright side of things. I wish I could,'' she finished with a sigh.

''You will,'' Judy prophesied. ''Just wait. Everything will be as rosy as this piece of cloth——''

''Oh, Judy!'' Miss Leonard cried. ''That's the dress I was wearing when John asked me to marry him. I promised him I would as soon as he came back from France, but he never came——''

She broke off with a sob.

The rest of them had been deeply moved by her story. How sad, Judy thought, that Miss Leonard had lost first her lover, then her friend, and now her voice. Instead of making her forget, as Judy had hoped it would, their adventure was only making her remember.

Red returned, the milk having been cared for.

''Still studying that quilt?'' he asked in a perplexed voice. ''I thought you intended to hunt up your grandmother's will.''

''We do,'' Judy assured him, looking up with misty eyes.

"Well, you won't find it in that quilt, I'm afraid."

"Won't we? I'm not so sure of that," she replied, turning to the others. "There's something very strange about all this. It wouldn't surprise me at all if the quilt did help us. Wasn't there a story somewhere about a deed being hidden in a quilt. Well, I feel somehow that something's hidden in this quilt—something important. I haven't studied it half as long as I would like to."

"If you think the will's sewed up inside it," Red suggested, "why don't you rip it apart?"

"Rip it!" Judy was horrified. "Rip this beautiful quilt, this quilt that Grandma spent half her life piecing together? Why, I'd just as soon—I'd just as soon rip off a finger," she declared fiercely. "Anyway, if she had sewed up the will inside the quilt—which is ridiculous—anyone could feel the paper crackle."

"The whole quilt crackles with all those notes pinned to it," Horace observed.

"Oh, look!" cried Honey, darting to pick up a piece of paper that fluttered to the floor as Judy held up the quilt.

"What is it?" everybody cried at once, gathering around her.

"It isn't the will," Honey answered, handing it to Judy. "It's only another note. It must have been pinned to the lining of the quilt. You read it."

"Dear Judy," she began reading. *"This is my memory quilt. I started it years ago when your mother was only a baby. She will remember every piece in it as I have saved patches from clothes worn both by my children and grandchildren. Patches from some of my dresses and your grandfather's shirts are also included, as well as pieces from dresses worn by friends of the family. The quilt is a family treasure as you will see when you read the notes I have pinned to the patches. Save the notes if you like but give the quilt to your mother——"*

"Judy!" Honey interrupted in dismay. "It isn't yours!"

"No, it's Mother's. But," Judy added, trying not to show her disappointment, "maybe she'll let me borrow it some time to—to study. I still think we may find a clue somewhere in the quilt."

CHAPTER IX

The Search Continues

"Now I'll tell you what I'd do if I was looking for clues," Red began importantly as Judy folded and put away the memory quilt, "I'd search those sewing machine drawers first thing——"

"We already did that," Honey interrupted. "We told you we found the playing cards in one of them. In fact, the very one where Judy thought she would find the will."

"That goes to show you what happened then," Red went on undaunted. "Someone did take the will out to make room for the cards, just like Horace said. It might have been Blackie or Button or either one of the two Fowler boys that was playing with us. I don't know. But it makes no difference anyhow. They didn't want the will. It was just in their way. They could have laid it on top of the sewing machine or maybe on one of the shelves in the pantry. Think I'll have a look."

"We all will," announced Horace motioning to the others. "Come on, folks, let's continue the search."

"I'll search the table here in the living room

72

where it's warm and comfortable," said Honey, opening the table drawer and taking out a stack of old letters and papers.

"I'll look through the desk," put in Miss Leonard. "That seems to me the logical place to put a will."

"Well, then, I shall explore the kitchen cabinet. Perhaps I'll find a cracker or two," Peter added. "Hamburgers aren't very filling. That was all Judy and I had for supper—a couple of hamburgers at Joe's."

"It wasn't the food. It was the atmosphere," laughed Judy who never thought of Joe's without remembering the day Peter gave her her engagement ring, an exquisite diamond in an antique setting. It had been in his family for years, just as her grandmother's things had been in hers, and because of that she treasured it all the more. She knew exactly where she would search—in the dish closet so that no one else would need to move or possibly break the precious Wedgwood china.

"If you find any food in there, let us know about it," Horace told her as she approached the closet. "We had a bite at home just before we started but that was four-thirty, a little early I thought. I could eat a steak——"

"Are we looking for the will or for something to eat?" asked Judy trying to sound severe and failing utterly.

"We might combine the two and eat while we

search,'' suggested Peter, opening the cabinet.
"Just as I thought! A box of crackers. Honey!"
he called in to the living room. "Would you and
Miss Leonard like something to eat?"

"No, thanks," Honey called back. "We aren't
hungry. Besides, we're busy looking through
these papers."

"I'm busy, too," Judy announced from the
high stool where she had climbed to search the top
shelves of the china closet.

She found a few packages of flower seeds tucked
in behind a teapot but nothing else that remotely
resembled a will.

"Did you find anything in the pantry?" she
called to Red who was rattling tins.

"No. Thought I'd pour out some of this milk
for you folks, since you all seem to be so hungry.
I remember how your grandmother always used to
offer you milk."

"Yes, she did, Red. Thanks for thinking of it,"
Judy answered as she climbed down for her glass
of milk.

Everyone felt refreshed. Red served the milk
on a tray, just as Grandmother Smeed used to do.
With it was the box of crackers so that those who
were hungry could help themselves. It was
thoughtful of Red. Judy could see he was doing
his best to make up for the worry he had caused.
He was now convinced it was his fault that the will
was missing.

"It's probably right in this kitchen in some easy place that we didn't think of looking," he said as he took out the tray filled with empty glasses. "Maybe I picked it up myself and put it some place. Gosh! Wouldn't I just be dumb enough to put it in the wastepaper basket?"

"Has it been emptied lately?" asked Peter.

"Nope. Not for a long time," Red replied, already dumping the contents on the floor.

Judy and Peter helped him sort the papers. Nothing of any value could be found.

"We'll just have to keep on looking," he said doggedly. "We can't accuse Blackie of taking it till we've searched the whole house. I can't see any sense in his wanting the will, anyhow, with everything peaceable in your family and no relations fighting over it."

"I can't either," Judy agreed. "It certainly would be a dumb idea trying to make us pay to get it back. Mother would see that Horace and I had whatever Grandma meant us to have, that is, if she knew."

"That's the deuce of it, not knowing," complained Horace. "She might have turned this house over to some institution for the care of destitute cats for all we can tell——"

"Horace, she wouldn't!"

"I know it," he agreed, "but she might have had some idea in her mind that none of us dreamed of. If we don't find the will——"

"But we *must* find it," interrupted Judy who was now searching frantically in every remote corner of the kitchen. "Maybe it fell down behind the baseboard or something. I notice it's loose."

"The entire house needs fixing up before it's fit for anyone to live in," declared Horace.

"We didn't finish cleaning up the plaster in Judy's room," Miss Leonard remembered, "but I suppose someone will have to come in and dust anyway after the ceiling's been fixed."

"And this wall too," Red added, knocking against the wall back of the sewing machine and rattling down some loose plaster. "Here's where the baseboard came loose."

"My goodness!" exclaimed Honey, peering over the top of the sewing machine. "A piece of paper could fall into that crack just as easily as not."

"It could slip right down over the edge of the sewing machine," Judy added. "Red, will you get a hammer?"

He left the room and returned with the hammer almost immediately. Peter took it and began to pry loose the baseboard. The nails squeaked like protesting mice as the claws of the hammer pulled them away from the wood. More plaster rattled down, sounding as though something alive were scurrying about behind the wall. Honey shivered and Miss Leonard held her ears.

"Here she comes!" announced Peter, giving one last tug.

"Look out!" warned Horace and Red as the baseboard swung away from the wall.

The others stepped back obediently, but Judy had caught a glimpse of something white behind the baseboard and reached for it just in time to received a sharp blow on her hand as the board snapped back into place.

"Ouch! There's a nail in that!" she cried out in pain.

"We told you to keep away——"

"Don't argue about it now," commanded Peter, grasping the board and pulling it away again. "Help me hold this," he told Horace. "There, Judy, is your hand free?"

"It's free, but do wait a minute," she pleaded. "There are some papers in here. They may be important papers. Please wait until I get them out."

"Your hand is bleeding," sympathized Honey.

"I'll get a bandage," offered Miss Leonard.

"It's really nothing—only a little scratch from the nail. But I suppose it ought to be bandaged," Judy agreed as she placed her handful of precious papers on the edge of the sewing machine. That seemed to her to be the proper place for them as her grandfather always used to bring in the mail and leave it there for her grandmother to read and sort. Peter grinned understandingly.

"Mustn't anybody touch those papers until Judy's hand is taken care of," he warned. "I think, since she was the one to be injured, she's earned the right to examine them first.''

"Thanks, Peter," murmured Judy from the sink where she was already bathing her badly scratched hand.

CHAPTER X

A Lost Message

THE bulky bandage on Judy's hand made the injury look worse than it was. It was her right hand too. But she always found something to be thankful for and this time it was the fact that the bandage wasn't on the hand that wore Peter's ring. Still it did make awkward work of sorting the papers she had found behind the baseboard.

"How do you suppose so many papers got down there?" asked Horace as he waited for Judy to divulge the contents of what she had found.

"Slipped down by accident most likely," she returned. "Here's a bargain sale that was held at Brandt's department store back in nineteen thirty. Goodness! Didn't girls wear their dresses long?"

"Oh, dear!" sighed Miss Leonard who was taking the looked-over papers as Judy handed them to her, "I thought surely that one would be the will."

"Just as I thought, it isn't here." And Judy was about to hand Miss Leonard a postal card, the last in the stack, when the words "Family Tree" caught her eye.

"Look! Isn't this cute?" she exclaimed, exhibiting the card. "It's supposed to be a family tree and all the leaves have faces."

"There's a verse too," Peter observed over her shoulder. "Read it, Judy. I like to hear you read."

"It isn't long. Just this." And she began reading:

> "A tiny bud has bloomed today
> Upon our family tree,
> And every branch and twig and stem
> Is happy as can be.
> It's a *girl*."

"Why, it's a birth announcement!" Honey exclaimed, her eyes widening in surprise.

"So it is! The word *girl* has been filled in with pen and ink. It's a little faded now. And look!" Judy went on excitedly as she turned the card over in her bandaged hand, "It's dated nineteen twenty-something. I can't quite make it out."

"Can you make out the message?" Peter questioned.

"Only a little. *anna* it looks like, but it's spelled with a small *a*. . . . *anna arrived this morning. She weighs seven pounds and* . . . See! That part's blurred. And then it says *But Lucy* . . .

"Judy! Are you sure it says that?" cried Miss Leonard, reaching for the card.

"Don't you think it does?"

"Oh, my dears!" exclaimed the music teacher, her eyes suddenly filling with tears. "Lucy had a baby and we never knew!"

There was a moment of awed silence as the meaning of the message became clear.

"Grandpa and Grandma must have had some reason for keeping it secret. But why?" Horace asked after a moment.

"Maybe because they didn't approve of Lucy's husband—" Peter began but Judy interrupted.

"No, it wasn't that either. I don't believe they knew! Just listen a minute and I'll tell you how I think it happened. This baseboard is right back of the sewing machine where Grandma used to sort the mail. The baseboard has probably been loose a long time and it would have been quite possible for the wind to have done this mischief all by itself. Grandpa hardly ever glanced at the mail, you know, until Grandma had seen it."

"But, Judy, they went to Lucy's funeral," protested Miss Leonard.

"Yes, and if they had known about the baby, they would have brought it home."

"Do you really think so?"

"I know it," Judy replied positively. "I just can't imagine Grandma leaving it to be brought up by Lucy's husband when she disapproved of him so. She would have made enough fuss so that everybody would have known about the baby, even if she hadn't been able to take it. After all, it was her own grandchild. She would have insisted upon seeing it if she had known."

"And now the baby must be almost grown up," Miss Leonard added. "Lucy died the spring after you were born, Judy."

"Then this girl must be nearly my age."

"Your own cousin," Honey put in, "and you've never seen her."

"I wonder if she knows about me," said Judy thoughtfully.

"It isn't very likely," Peter reasoned, "or she would have been in touch with you. Cousins are close enough to want to know each other, I should think. What do you think about it, Red?" he asked, turning to the hired man who had said nothing about the discovery but who appeared to be deep in thought.

"Well," said Red, shoving his hands deep in his pockets and looking as impressive as he knew how, "I was just changing my mind about everything being peaceable in your family and no relations fighting over the will."

"What do you mean?" gasped Judy. "You don't think my cousin——"

"Aw now, don't you go defending your cousin when you don't even know who she is," Red broke in. "Like as not you wouldn't have much use for her, anyhow. And if her old man's a crook, as you say, I wouldn't put it past him to do away with the will so's the kid could get her half——"

"Would it be as much as that?" asked Honey to whom law was a complete puzzle.

"I'm afraid it would," Peter agreed. "When there is no will children share equally in the estate and a grandchild whose mother is dead takes the share the mother would have received. Yes, I'm afraid it's pretty plain what's happening. Your uncle by marriage is trying to gain possession of half your grandmother's property. If he succeeds, the place will have to be sold in order to be divided. There will be no way out of it."

"Oh, dear! What a mess!" sighed Judy. "Just when I was thinking it would be so nice to have a cousin my own age so that she could spend holidays with us as one of the family—but I guess that was just a pipe dream. I probably wouldn't like her if I knew her, with a crook for a father——"

"She had Lucy for a mother," Miss Leonard broke in gently.

"I know. And I would like to meet her. I do wish someone remembered the name of the man Lucy married."

"Your mother might remember it," Miss Leonard began. "But wait! Here's an even better suggestion. I found an old album in the desk and it's filled with family pictures and records. I'll get it."

"We might all find it more comfortable in the living room by the fire," said Horace, leading the way. "I'll throw on another log. There! Isn't that just right for reminiscing?"

"Reminiscing!" laughed Honey as Miss Leonard spread the album before them. "I hope you don't think we're old enough to remember this!"

The picture she pointed out was a tintype taken of Grandpa and Grandma Smeed when they were first married. It was faintly colored and Grandma was wearing one of the prints in the quilt. The dress was all ruffles and braid with a high lace collar. Grandpa's collar and his moustache nearly met.

In another picture Grandma Smeed was a little girl with a china-headed doll. That reminded Judy that the doll was still in existence. It was one of a collection of rare old dolls that were kept in the lower part of the china closet. Judy had seen them when she was hunting for the will.

More and more pictures followed. Great-aunts, great-uncles—all dead now. One of Mrs. Bolton's sisters who had died in early childhood, Uncle John in his soldier's uniform and then Lucy.

Judy held the album closer, studying her face. Her head was tilted a little in a defiant attitude. Her nose turned up almost as saucily as Judy's own.

"What color was her hair?" asked Judy. "It looks as though it might have been auburn like mine."

"The picture makes it appear darker than it really was," Miss Leonard answered. "No, Judy, it wasn't like yours. It was light brown, something the color of your mother's hair. But Lucy did resemble you in other ways. I always thought you took after your mother's people, Judy."

"I get my gray eyes from Dad," she declared proudly.

"It's funny about looks, isn't it? I was reading a book about heredity," Horace told them, "and it said that some traits skip a generation, so that a child is often more like its grandmother, or maybe its great-aunt, than it is like its own mother."

"I guess I took my hair from my Great-Aunt Belinda, if I had one," laughed Judy. "Mother says no one else in the family had hair in the least like mine, and Dad says it doesn't come from his side, either."

"Gosh! We were all redheads in my family," Red boasted. "There were ten of us and the teacher used to say she could spot a Burnett like a house afire, both by the color and the trouble he made. You see, I was sorta born to make trouble, I guess. We all gave our folks plenty of trouble—but what a jolly bunch when we got together!"

"Ten of you!" Judy exclaimed. "I should think you would be. And here Horace and I are without anybody except a cousin we never knew existed until this day. I can't even find any family record."

"Here it is," Miss Leonard pointed out, turning to the back of the album.

"*Lucy Smeed, married* . . . And they left the

rest blank," Judy said in disappointment. "On the next line is the date of her death but nothing about a baby. I'm sure Grandma couldn't have known a thing about my cousin Anna—if that's her name."

"The whole thing's so blurred one can make very little sense out of it," observed Horace, studying the card Judy had found.

"I think, if we could read it," Judy ventured, "that it would say, 'But Lucy is very ill' or 'is not expected to live' or something like that. We can see it must have said that. According to this record she died when the baby was two weeks old."

"And Heaven only knows who brought up the poor little thing or what kind of girl she is now," said Miss Leonard, closing the album with a hopeless gesture.

"There's one thing," Peter observed, "it certainly looks as though we won't find the will tonight. And I'm afraid, Judy, if you do meet your cousin, it will be in an unpleasant legal tangle over your grandmother's property."

Judy looked up from the postal card, her eyes alight with a new idea.

"Oh, I'm not so sure of that, Peter. Remember what you told the G-man? You said there might be another girl who looks like me. And Horace said people sometimes resembled their great-aunts more than their own mothers. So why couldn't cousins who took after the same great-aunt, for instance, look alike? And if there is another girl who looks like me and the pocketbook was intended for her, why then I may meet her at the lecture next Tuesday night and——"

"What lecture?" interrupted Peter, looking bewildered.

"Why, the one Horace is going to find out about," Judy answered.

"Judy, are you crazy or am I?" her brother asked, rumpling his hair to make it look wild.

Honey let out a little scream of laughter.

"She's trying to say that if she has a cousin and if the cousin looks like her and if the pocketbook was intended for the cousin and if she's at the lecture and if we can find out what lecture it is and if——"

"Honey, for goodness sake, stop before you have us all crazy," commanded Peter. "The more *ifs* you put in, the more complicated this sounds when it may really be a simple matter of Judy's uncle by marriage trying to get possession of the will for his daughter."

"Then where does Blackie fit in?" asked Red.

"And the lecture?" questioned Horace. "I'm pretty keen on attending some lecture Tuesday night, if only to be there when things start popping——"

But the clock on the mantel, striking midnight, drowned out the rest of what he was trying to say.

"Mother is going to think something happened to us!" cried Judy, jumping up with a start for none of them had given a thought to the time.

"Well, didn't it?" drawled Red as they prepared to leave.

CHAPTER XI

An Unknown Cousin

On the way home Judy was silent and thoughtful. If she had a cousin her own age she certainly wanted to meet her. She was prepared to like her whatever her father might have done.

"It wasn't her fault," she thought, "and anyway, maybe he wasn't so terrible. Just because Grandpa and Grandma disapproved of him——"

"Peter," she asked aloud, "what do you suppose her father could have done to make them hate him so?"

"Who's father? What's this?" asked Peter startled out of his own thoughts.

"Why, my cousin Anna's. I mean, why did Grandpa and Grandma hate her father——"

"Oh, the man Lucy married? I couldn't say, I'm sure. I thought our family was mixed up once but I must say, Judy, yours is in nearly as bad a mess as mine ever was. We were tied up with the Thompson gang by marriage but it's beginning to look as though you might be tied up with Blackie——"

"Really, Peter?" She sank back in the car seat, tired and disgusted. "Oh, dear! I guess it

89

does. I had another theory, but it's too impractical to be worth much. I borrowed it from you and even the G-man wouldn't take it seriously."

"You mean the theory that the note Blackie gave you was really intended for someone who looks like you?"

"Yes, my cousin Anna. I believe she's the girl the florist saw and also the girl who was supposed to receive that note in the black patent leather pocketbook. I can't believe it was meant for me, because I didn't intend to be at any lecture Tuesday night and she probably did."

"Where does the missing will come in then?" asked Peter.

"That's easy," Judy replied. "The information that might be worth a fortune was probably information about the will."

"I'd hardly say your grandmother's property was worth a fortune, Judy. And half of it would be worth only a couple of thousand dollars at the most."

"Property's going up in value now that Roulsville is booming."

"But not that much."

"Blackie may have exaggerated then. Or maybe there's a gold mine or something on the property——"

"A gold mine! That's good," laughed Peter. "You'll be discovering diamonds next."

"I guess I am foolish," she admitted. "If I discovered my cousin it would be about all I'd want."

"When she's probably responsible for this whole mess and the lost will included? The chances are that she will discover you when your grandmother's property comes up for distribution," Peter prophesied grimly as he turned his car into the garage driveway.

The other half of the garage was occupied by Dr. Bolton's car. Horace's rattletrap runabout was already parked on what he called "the fill," a piece of filled-in land where an old factory building had once stood. Now it was used as parking space by the poorer families who lived in the row of factory-built houses farther up Grove Street. These people, like the wealthy residents who lived on the fashionable end of the street, were the doctor's patients and Judy had done much to erase the old dividing line. People were all just people to her and whether they were rich or poor, fortunate or unfortunate, she always thought of them as having the same feelings that she had.

Thus Judy could not think of her unknown cousin as anything but a healthy, vivacious, adventure-loving girl like herself. She tried to imagine how it might have changed her character if she had not had the guidance of a loving mother, and if her father had been engaged in some crooked business, instead of being the kindly doctor that he was.

"I'd still be worth something," she thought. "I wouldn't be all bad and I don't believe my cousin Anna is either."

Judy's mother had been waiting up for her. Blackberry, also keeping vigil, was perched on the window sill. He came forth and stretched himself as Judy reached down to pat him.

"You're awfully late," Mrs. Bolton said. "Horace got in half an hour ago with Miss Leonard and he had already taken Honey home."

"That just goes to prove that Peter is a more cautious driver," laughed Judy. "Besides, we had a great deal to talk about."

"Linda told me you couldn't find the will."

"Was that all she told you, Mother?"

"About all," she admitted. "She seemed very tired and said her head ached, and Horace didn't say much either. I didn't question him because I know how early he has to be down at the newspaper office. He needs his rest and so do you, Judy. I can't imagine what kept you so long."

"I'll tell you in the morning," Judy promised but, as she picked up Blackberry to put him out for the night, her mother noticed her bandaged hand.

"You've hurt yourself!" she exclaimed in dismay. "Come, Judy girl, tell me about it now. I won't sleep unless you do. I could tell by the way Horace acted that something had gone wrong.''

"I'm not so sure about that. Anyway," Judy answered lightly, "I'm not so terribly injured. It's just a scratch where I knocked my hand against a nail. The baseboard came loose in Grandma's kitchen and I reached behind it to get this.''

And Judy placed the card which she had brought home with her in her mother's hands.

"What on earth!" exclaimed Mrs. Bolton, glancing at the picture of the family tree.

"Read what it says," Judy directed her.

She read the verse, turned the card over, and then excused herself to get the glasses she used for close reading. She studied both the back and the face of the card through the glasses as though she were unable to believe what she saw.

"Where did you say you found this?" she asked Judy at last.

"Behind the baseboard back of Grandma's sewing machine. But tell me what you think it means, Mother.''

"I can hardly believe it! It must mean that my sister Lucy had a baby girl just before she died. But it seems impossible that your grandmother wouldn't have taken the child to bring up—or, at least, told us about it. You're not fooling me, are you, Judy? This isn't any kind of a joke?''

"Now, Mother," she chided, "do you think I

would fool you about anything as serious as this? The baby is my own cousin and I intend to do whatever I can to find her.''

''But wouldn't that be impossible after all this time has gone by?''

''I don't think so, Mother. Even though we didn't know about the baby she must have known about us. At least, her father did. I wish some-one could remember his name.''

''Your grandmother never mentioned his last name. His first name was Henry, but I'm afraid that won't help much and the signature on the card is quite unreadable. If Linda doesn't re-member his full name, then I'm afraid no one does. She was at your grandmother's house more than I was in those days, for Lucy ran away several years after your father and I were mar-ried.''

''Tell me what you know about the man she ran away with,'' begged Judy.

''But I know nothing except that your grand-parents disapproved of anyone who made his living fooling the public or cheating the public. I don't remember which they said. They also spoke of Lucy not being responsible for what she did. They said this man had tricked her into marrying him when she was not herself. But really, dear,'' her mother finished, ''I'm only con-fusing you. It was all so confusing. Hasn't Miss Leonard told you anything?''

"She told me all she knew, I guess," Judy admitted. "But it does seem as though someone in the family would have remembered his name."

"But none of us knew him, Judy girl. Lucy met him secretly. No one had any idea she intended to run away with him. Then one morning her bed was empty and a note pinned on the pillow said, 'Henry and I were married last night. Sorry we had to do it without your consent. Some day you will understand and forgive your Lucy.' It was the last note we ever had from her. You may find it somewhere among your grandmother's things. It shocked us so much that every one of us knew it by heart. Your grandmother was ready to forgive Lucy for anything, but I doubt if she knew her husband's whole name until the day he telephoned that Lucy was dead."

"Oh," said Judy. "He telephoned? Then there wouldn't be any chance of finding the letter that told about her death."

"I'm afraid not, dear. It all happened so long ago and, not knowing about the baby, none of us saw any reason for getting in touch with Lucy's husband. As your grandmother once said, 'It isn't as though he were a man of honor.'"

"Dear me!" sighed Judy. "I wish I could have found this card before Grandma's death. I don't think she knew about the baby, either."

"It's quite possible that she didn't," Mrs. Bolton agreed. "The card could have been lost the day it came. Imagine the difference if she had known! Why, you two girls might have been brought up together. I would have been glad to take Lucy's baby."

"I know. It's sad, isn't it? Just one little postcard being lost probably changed my cousin Anna's whole life. Peter thinks I wouldn't like her if I knew her now."

"You might not, dear."

"I know, Mother, but it isn't all in bringing up —What was that old verse Grandma used to say?"

> "It isn't all in bringing up,
>   Let folks say what they will.
>   If you silver scour a pewter cup,
>   It will be pewter still."

"That's it!" Judy exclaimed when her mother had finished quoting. "And don't you think it's the other way around, too? Some of the fine traits of our family were born in Anna and no matter who brought her up they must still be there."

"Like Honey," said Mrs. Bolton thoughtfully. "She was brought up by strangers, too. But she was a sweet girl in spite of it and fitted into her own family as nicely as though she had always lived with them."

"We found her in time, that's why," Judy

agreed. "Oh, Mother! We must find my cousin.
It may be that we can make up for all the years we
haven't known her. Even if we do have to sell
Grandma's house, having a real cousin like other
girls will be worth it. Maybe it could be arranged
so that we could keep the family treasures and
just let them have the property. The house needs
replastering anyway. But there was a whole
chest full of treasures that Grandma had packed
away. She marked Grandpa's ivory chessmen for
Horace and her needle paintings for Linda——"

"Miss Leonard, dear. She's older than you
are."

"But she asked me to call her Linda. And
besides," Judy went on, "there was the most
beautiful patchwork quilt in the chest. Grandma
called it her memory quilt and I simply love it.
It is made of the pieces from special dresses and
things that we all wore. There are patches from
Grandma's dresses and yours and mine and ever
so many others. There is one from Linda's
dress with the blue stars that she wore when she
first sang in the choir and a piece from that lovely
butterfly print that Lucy wore the day she ran
away."

"I remember helping her make that dress,"
said Mrs. Bolton softly. "What else?"

"Lots more pieces and a note that said the quilt
was yours."

"And was there nothing for you, Judy?"

"No. Nothing. Maybe Grandma intended to put something in for me and then forgot. Anyway, you'll let me borrow the memory quilt sometimes, won't you, Mums?"

"Of course, darling. Now run upstairs and try to get some rest before daylight."

"I will." And, kissing her mother, Judy ran to her room. She crawled into bed still wondering about her cousin Anna—a girl about her own age who looked so much like her that they might have been taken for twins if they had been brought up together.

"I made a fool blunder," Sam Tucker said again in her thoughts, "called out 'Hello, Judy!' to a girl who was driving through here with her folks . . ."

"Her folks," thought Judy sleepily. "She has folks then. Maybe some nice family adopted her. I'll ask the florist about it tomorrow," she decided as she drifted off to sleep.

CHAPTER XII

A Suspected Plot

"Her folks? You mean the folks that was with that girl I mistook for you?"

It was Sam Tucker's voice answering the question Judy had asked him over the telephone.

"Yes. Tell me what they looked like, all about them," Judy urged. "Someone mistook me for some other girl and I'm trying to find her."

"So I heard. A young man named Trent was in here questioning me. Well, there was her little brother—a freckle-faced boy of about ten and a couple of sisters or friends, I don't know which. But I know the boy was her brother. I heard him call her 'Sis'."

"And what about her father? Was he with them?"

"He didn't come in," the florist replied. "I glanced at him sitting there in the car. It was a fancy limousine, but he was driving it. There wasn't a chauffeur. I only saw the side of his face and he looked just like anybody else."

"But everybody looks different," Judy protested.

"Well, this man didn't. He looked just like a dozen other men."

"Was he young?"

"Middle-aged, I would say."

"Was he dark or light?"

"Oh, about medium."

Judy closed the conversation, seeing that it was useless to question the florist further, and turned to her brother who always seemed to be near by when she made important calls.

"Get anything out of him?" he asked her casually.

"Not much. I may be wrong about that girl being my cousin," Judy admitted. "It seems she has a bunch of brothers and sisters."

"That lets her out completely, I should think."

"Well, unless she was adopted——"

"But why would they adopt a girl if they already had a family of their own?"

"The answer is, they wouldn't. But I'm going to the lecture, anyway, and see if there is anyone there who looks like me."

"Don't start talking to any mirrors," Horace advised as he started for the newspaper office.

"I won't," she called after him, "and remember, you're to look up the lectures!"

She couldn't hear him answer, but he gave a sign that meant he understood. Then it was time for Judy to be thinking about her office too. Peter called for her a few minutes later and she spent the morning trying to concentrate on first mort-

gages, for much of Peter's business had to do with
the legal end of real estate.

Mr. Trent came in shortly after ten o'clock and
wanted to hear all the latest developments in what
he called 'The case of the patent leather pocketbook.' Peter had telephoned him earlier saying he
had a new tip on Blackie. Now he advised him to
have a talk with Red.

"Aren't you going to tell him about the missing
will?" Judy questioned.

"I'm afraid Mr. Trent wouldn't be interested,"
Peter began but the G-man interrupted.

"A missing will, did you say? Now we have
something definite to fit in with that note. If
Blackie has information, as the note says, he probably stole the will and expects you to pay for its
return."

"Then you don't think he would have destroyed
the will?" asked Judy anxiously.

"He might have if some other relative paid him
to do it. Is anyone else trying to get hold of the
property?"

"We hope not," Judy answered. "But last
night we discovered that there is a first cousin who
would have a legal right to half of it if the will isn't
found."

Peter added a few details about their search
through the sewing machine drawers, and finally
Red's confession that Blackie, who had entered
the house supposedly to play cards, had access to
the drawer where the will was kept.

"Then," declared Mr. Trent, "it's as plain as the nose on your face. Blackie is holding the will to see who will give him the most money for it. He doesn't care whether you pay to get it or whether this cousin of yours pays to have it destroyed. You see, Miss Bolton, it's money he's after. Tearing up a will would be just like tearing up a piece of blank paper to a crook like that."

"But we have to keep him from tearing it up. We have to get possession of it somehow."

"There's just one wise way to do that, Miss Bolton, and that's to trap Blackie."

"I know," she answered. "I'm going to help if I can. I'm going to attend a lecture——"

"Better report it to us so that one of our men can go along with you," the G-man advised, "and don't take any money with you. You'll lose it if you do."

"I won't," she promised.

"Now suppose you tell me how you know what lecture to attend."

"I don't." She hesitated. She could tell by the expression on his face that he didn't believe her. "I told you my brother was going to look up some lectures. I'll attend one, that's all. I don't know which one."

"Now look here, Miss Bolton," the G-man said in a firm voice, "if you want the government's help, you'll have to tell everything you know. We can't have an agent there to help you unless we know where you're going."

"But I don't know where I'm going myself,"
she protested weakly.

"That's right. She doesn't," Peter defended
her. "She intends to take a chance and attend
some lecture just to see if anything happens."

The G-man grinned.

"That's what she told you. Well, so long.
Thanks for the tip about Blackie, Mr. Dobbs. I'll
see your friend Red Burnett."

Peter gave him directions to the house in Dry
Brook Hollow and in a moment more he was on his
way.

"He didn't believe us!" gasped Judy as he
closed the door.

"And is it any wonder? It certainly does look
queer," Peter declared. "There may be a dozen
lectures in a dozen different towns on Tuesday
night. We'd be almost certain to attend the
wrong one, waste an evening and our own time, as
well as the time of Uncle Sam's G-men."

"Then let's each attend a different lecture,"
Judy suggested. "With Horace and Honey and
Miss Leonard and maybe Red and some of our
other friends to help us, we could cover every lecture within a hundred miles of here. That's the
way reporters do when they scent a good story."

"And when they have enough reporters," Peter
added. But he agreed to the plan and that evening Horace had the first of many lecture notices
to exhibit.

"Well, Judy," he announced, spreading the no-

tices before her on the living room table, "the Farringdon Historical Society has a meeting on Tuesday night and the public is invited. There will be
a lecture——"

"Really?" she interrupted excitedly. "What
about?"

"About the history of the county, I presume,
and dry as a bone."

"Anything else?"

"Here's one in Emporium. The garden club is
going to have a lecture on spring flowers with lantern slides——"

"Lantern slides! I thought they went out of
style with hoopskirts and pantalettes."

"Well, be that as it may, it's Emporium and
Blackie may attend. Furthermore, the Parent-
Teachers Association of Emporium is having a
talk on *The Unusual Child*."

"Get Mother to go to that one," Judy advised
laughingly. "She may find out something about
us."

"Frankly," Horace told her, "at this rate we'll
be scheduled to attend at least twenty lectures and,
unless we divide ourselves like amoebas, we can't
possibly do it."

"I know it. We'll just have to pick out the most
likely ones and distribute them among our
friends," Judy said. "That historical society lecture is one I'd leave out."

"That's the boss' pet hobby."

"I know. Mr. Lee and a lot of other aristocratic old gentlemen will attend. But no girl that looks like me——"

"You still have that idea?"

"It's pretty well squelched by now," Judy admitted. "But I was going to add, 'and no Blackie.' He's really the one we're looking for."

"It would be just our luck to pick the wrong lecture. Well, tomorrow night," Horace promised, "I may have more. At least it gives us something to think about."

Judy held her head in her hands and moaned.

"Some day," she told her brother, "I'm going to take a vacation from thinking. My brain's in a whirl now and by the time we've picked out the right lecture *and* listened to it, well, I leave it to you. Will my poor brain need a rest or won't it?"

"And what about mine?"

"If any," laughed Judy, but the fond look she gave her brother took the sting from her words. It was really good of him to go to so much trouble for her. He'd do it, she knew, whether or not there was the possibility of a story for the paper.

CHAPTER XIII

Hypnotism, Its Use and Misuse

The following evening Judy met the two chums, Lois and Lorraine, and assigned a lecture to them. They said they'd be glad to look out for a girl who resembled Judy and a man who fitted the description she gave them of Blackie. This was not the first mystery they had helped Judy solve and Arthur Farringdon-Pett, Lois' brother, said he would be glad to drive to a near-by town where a lecture on psychology was being given.

"Lorraine and I are going to need to know how to get along with people, and with each other," he added humorously. "We expect to be married in June. Lorraine said you and Peter might join us and make it a double wedding."

"That would be lovely," Judy exclaimed, delighted that Arthur had suggested it. "I'll have to straighten out this mess about the threatening note first and then I'll talk it over with Peter."

"Do you think there's any real danger?" Arthur asked anxiously.

"Of course not," she laughed. "There's a mistake somewhere, that's all. I'm not the type of person to be frightened by notes. There was no threat in it anyway—only a picture of a gun from some child's toy stamp set. It's really the loss of Grandma's will that I'm worried about.''

''But you have G-men on the case.''

''I know it. Blackie is wanted for more serious crimes. That's why. They're not chasing him simply because he wrote that note. Besides, blackmail is a federal offense. Otherwise I'd have turned the note over to Chief Kelly here in Farringdon. At least he knows me well enough to believe what I tell him.''

''Don't the G-men?''

''No. They think I'm lying because I'm afraid to tell the truth. And they think I know what lecture I'm going to attend when I still can't decide. Maybe Horace will bring home some more lecture notices tonight.''

''We'll help you with them if he does,'' Arthur assured her as they parted at the gate of the Farringdon-Pett estate.

True to her predictions, there were more notices. Judy's many friends and acquaintances were all willing to help. Red rounded up two of his brothers in a not too distant town and chose a talk on landscaping the country home which he wished to attend himself.

''Might as well learn something about my own business while I'm at it,'' he commented with a grin.

Honey discovered a lecture on art that she really

wanted to attend, and Selma Brady, one of Judy's younger friends, promised to listen to a talk on organizing a choral group. Both these lectures were being given right in Farringdon and were, Peter contended, reasonably safe. The one he chose for himself was not so safe and Judy was not surprised that he hesitated about permitting her to go with him. It was to be held in a tent, set up for the purpose, at the edge of a deep woods just outside the town of Emporium. The lecture was on *Crime and the Criminal*, a subject which would be quite likely to appeal to Blackie. Peter was fairly certain this was the lecture referred to in the note.

The Community Hall in Roulsville featured a lecture on travel and Judy prevailed upon the Piper family to attend that.

"Now," she declared as the last of her friends departed with their lecture notices, "we'll have to scare up a few more people to cover these." And she indicated what appeared to be four or five additional notices at the bottom of the stack Horace had brought in.

"It isn't *these*. It's *this*," he declared. "The biggest and the best of the lecture notices. Feast your eyes upon the handsome job of printing. It was fate, no less, that sent this to the *Herald* office." And he unfolded an immense poster which read:

HYPNOTISM,

Its Use and Misuse

Learn the truth about the power of suggestion! Dr. Zoller, the greatest living authority on hypnotism, is touring the country! Don't miss his illuminating talk!

Come! Be educated! Be hypnotized!

Subjects Will Be Chosen from the Audience . . .

"That's the lecture I'll attend," Judy declared, eyes shining. "I've always wanted to be hypnotized."

"But, Sis, it's nowhere near Emporium and the chances are that it isn't the right lecture——"

"I know. The chances are that none of them are the right lectures. Where are you going, Horace?"

"Oh, I suppose I may as well see the lantern slides and drive Mom to this Parents' Association thing. That will cover two of them."

"Poor Horace!" sympathized Judy. "Well, there's one thing. If I attend the hypnotism lecture, at least I won't be bored."

"But who'll take you if Peter goes to the one on *Crime and the Criminal?*"

Judy hadn't thought of that. It would be nice if she had a car of her own, now that Peter had taught her how to drive. But she had to admit that she still felt safer with him at the wheel. She would daydream and forget to watch the road and her father had never yet trusted her at the wheel of his car.

"Maybe Dad will take me."

"Try it. But I'm warning you," her brother said, "he'll be too busy. And you can't persuade Peter not to attend the one on *Crime and the Criminal*. He's certain Blackie will be there."

"I wish I were as certain of that," Judy returned as, with the notice in her hand, she rapped softly on the door of her father's office. Although it was long after office hours, he was still there working on his records.

"Come in," he called in a professional voice which changed the moment he saw it was Judy who had rapped.

"Well, I hear you're covering all the lectures within a radius of a hundred miles. What's this? A new one."

"Horace brought it in. It was at the bottom of the stack," Judy said, placing the poster on her father's desk. "Doesn't it look interesting, Dad? And a doctor is giving the talk. I'd love to go."

"Hypnotism? Hmmm!" said Dr. Bolton and for a long time he said nothing more. He simply sat there staring at the notice and drumming the end of his pencil thoughtfully against the edge of his desk.

"Dr. Zoller? He's an important man," he said at last. "I shouldn't mind hearing him myself. This man has done wonders, Judy girl. There's an article about some of his marvelous cures in one of my medical journals. Cases that baffle the ordinary doctor are his specialty. He works on the theory that a semi-conscious mind is a receptive mind—But you wouldn't understand all that," he broke off. "The thing of it is, can we get Linda to go?"

"Linda? But it was you I wanted to go with me, Dad."

"Unfortunately, that is impossible. I have to be at the hospital to assist with a delicate eye operation," the doctor said. "But there must be some way to take Linda. This may be the answer to her whole problem. What's Peter doing with his car?"

"He's driving it to a lecture on *Crime and the Criminal.*"

"And Horace?"

"He's driving to two lectures."

"I suppose you wouldn't call on Arthur."

"I already have. He and Lorraine are driving to one lecture while Lois and Donald Carter attend another. You see, all the cars are taken."

"Well then, Judy girl, I'll advance the fare if you go by train. This lecture is important. I don't think there's a chance that it's the lecture you're looking for, but Dr. Zoller is the one man I know about who might help Linda. But first she must consent to be one of his subjects."

"Dad, I'm afraid I don't understand you," Judy said in bewilderment. "I came in here to ask you if I might go to this lecture and now you're practically telling me I must go. But what I don't see is how a hypnotist can help Linda. Hypnotists put people to sleep, don't they? Or they make them go into sort of a trance. What good could that do?"

"I'm not promising that it would do any good, but Linda is my patient," the doctor replied, "and therefore I must make every effort to help her. Hypnotism may help where medicine has failed. Anyway, it's worth trying. Look up train schedules and hotels. You'll have to spend the night in Westlake. It says at the bottom of the poster that that's the town where the lecture is being held."

"It's a college town, isn't it Dad?" asked Judy.

"Yes, and Westlake is a fine college. Your mother and I hoped you might go there some day, but I suppose you're learning just as much working for Peter."

"And talking with you," she added. "I never knew before that hypnotism was a real science that interested doctors. I thought it was fake like magic."

"You'll see whether or not it's fake," Dr. Bolton prophesied, "when you hear Dr. Zoller. I've never met the man, but I've read his articles and they're brilliant. If Linda hesitates about going, send her in to me and I'll have a talk with her."

"All right, Dad. I will. But my goodness! I never thought you'd be the one to send me to a lecture on hypnotism. Excuse me if I seem a little foggy. I'm still getting used to the idea."

On the way out of her father's office Judy almost bumped into her mother who was just coming in.

"There!" she announced, turning to him. "Didn't I tell you I was foggy? I couldn't even see Mother. To tell you the truth, Dad, I'm almost hypnotized at the thought of this lecture."

"Hypnotized!" exclaimed Mrs. Bolton, standing perfectly still in the doorway.

"She's going to a lecture on hypnotism. That's all," Dr. Bolton explained. "Linda is going with her, if you two can persuade her to do so."

"Indeed I shall not persuade her or anybody to attend such a lecture," said Mrs. Bolton, stiffening and looking very determined. "For once, I'm going to disagree with you," she said to the doctor. "There's no need for Judy or Linda or any responsible person to be interested in a lecture on any such crazy subject. I declare, I don't know what you're thinking of. And Judy, if you do go, you'll be doing it against my wishes. Do you understand?"

"But Dad asked me to," Judy protested, surprised that her mild-mannered little mother should have taken this sudden stand against him.

"Your father doesn't know what he's doing

then," Mrs. Bolton declared still more surprisingly. "Believe me, Judy girl, I wouldn't make the least objection if I didn't know the possible outcome. Don't you realize that once you are hypnotized you are no longer responsible for your actions? You are under the direction of your master, the hypnotist. Why, I read a story once about a subject who was induced to go on a shoplifting expedition for her master. And you must know the story of poor Trilby and the wicked Svengali. I'll never forget those burning eyes——"

"Where did you see them, Mother?"

"A long time ago in a silent picture. But it impressed me more than any of these modern screen stories because it was based on something which I knew to be true."

Judy turned appealingly to her father.

"Well, Mother doesn't seem to like the idea," she said.

"I never thought we'd meet opposition from you, my dear," the doctor said kindly to his wife. "This man is no criminal hypnotist such as you imagine. He is a noted physician and it was because I hoped that he might help Linda——"

"Through hypnotism?" Mrs. Bolton interrupted almost hysterically. "I'm sure Linda would rather never sing again!"

"But Mother. Dad knows. Dad is a doctor."

"I know, too." Mrs. Bolton picked up the notice. "And it says here that subjects will be chosen

from the audience. Suppose they chose you,
Judy? Suppose you ran away as your Aunt Lucy
did and we never saw you again. Your grandmother would turn over in her grave if she heard
of this. She said herself that Lucy never would
have done what she did if she hadn't been hypnotized!''

"She said that!" gasped Judy. "Then I must
go, Mother. I must find out."

"Wait a minute, Judy girl," urged the doctor.
"Don't you think it might be better if your mother
and I came to an understanding first?"

Judy nodded, too confused to speak, and almost
stumbled out of the door. She could hear her
mother sobbing, a thing that never happened.
Her parents had never disagreed before.

Cuddling Blackberry for comfort, Judy sank
into a chair in the living room and waited. Would
she go to the lecture or wouldn't she? And how
could Lucy have been hypnotized? Could this
hypnotist be in any way connected with the crook,
Blackie? If so, Judy was not at all sure she
wanted to attend the lecture for, if there was one
thing she valued above another, it was her ability
to think and reason for herself. She shuddered to
think of what might happen if she were hypnotized . . .

"Why, I'd be no better than a dog following his
master around," she murmured. At the word
"dog" Blackberry's tail bristled. "You don't

like the idea either, do you, Blackberry?'' she said, stroking him.

"Crook! Swindler!" croaked Horace's parrot sleepily from his cage in the corner.

Judy thought of Dr. Zoller. Was he really the eminent physician her father believed him to be or could it be that the bird was right?

CHAPTER XIV

JUDY'S DOUBLE

JUDY never knew exactly what was said behind the door of her father's office that evening for she dozed in the chair and it was Horace, coming in to cover the parrot, who roused her. But the following day Dr. and Mrs. Bolton were both agreed. Judy would be permitted to attend the lecture.

Miss Leonard, who regularly shopped on Saturday whether or not she was in need of new clothes, had spent the afternoon at Brandt's department store trying on new hats. She came home in a gay mood, a pert little pink straw creation perched on top her head.

"You look all ready to go places," Judy greeted her, "and I have some place to go. Were you ever in Westlake, the college town? Well, we're going to spend a day and a night there and attend a lecture in the college auditorium."

"I expected as much," laughed Miss Leonard. "You should start a detective agency, Judy. Your friends are all so willing to work for you."

"Are you willing too?" asked Judy. "It means five hours on the train, there and back, and a night in a hotel."

"I shall love it. How many are going?"

"Just you and me. The others are all going to attend lectures at other places. I've tried to cover them all."

"And succeeded beautifully," Miss Leonard added.

To Judy's relief, she didn't ask any more about the lecture and, although Judy meant to tell her it was a talk on hypnotism, she kept putting it off. And the longer she put it off the harder it was to tell.

On Monday she rode to the office with Peter and spent all day typing and taking notes, preparing for the two-day vacation he had promised her. No more was heard from Mr. Trent and Judy decided that she and Peter had bothered him enough. After all, she reasoned, the government had important things to do and Blackie was just one of many criminals who were at large.

At first Peter seemed a little disappointed because Judy had been the one to decide not to attend the lecture on *Crime and the Criminal* with him.

"It's sure to be good," he told her, "and we're much more apt to locate Blackie in Emporium than we are in Westlake. The college town, I should think, is much too far away to be considered. What made you decide to go there?"

"Something Dad said," Judy replied evasively. She would not, for the world, tell Peter of her mother's fears, or he too might object to the trip. Hypnotism was something, he said, in which he had never been very interested.

"It's probably all fake," he declared. "Such things usually are. But it's an exciting theme and will probably draw a big crowd. You're right, Judy. It is one of the lectures which we ought to cover."

Miss Leonard had little curiosity about the lecture. Still Judy put off showing her the notice which said subjects would be chosen from the audience.

Tuesday morning dawned bright and sunny. It was really the first warm spring day and, although Easter was still three weeks away, Miss Leonard thought her new hat would be suitable for the trip.

"I wish I had a new one," said Judy. "But perhaps I'll buy one in Westlake. We'll have plenty of time to kill. Our train leaves at ten and the lecture isn't until evening."

"That will give us time to stroll around the campus and see the college buildings," Miss Leonard told her enthusiastically as they packed their bags.

Judy took a fresh dress along to wear to the lecture, some clean underthings and her pajamas. That was all she would need for the short time they were staying. Her light tan coat was warm and would be just the thing in case it turned colder.

"Ready?" she asked slipping into it and then

pulling on a small beret. "I can pack this," she explained, "in case I buy a new hat."

Peter drove them to the station.

"I wish I could take you all the way," he remarked, "but it's a peculiar thing about the human animal. He can't be in more than one place at a time."

"We understand," Judy told him. She settled herself in the green plush seat beside Miss Leonard and accepted the magazine Peter had brought along for her. "It's going to be fun on the train, anyway. It's been so long since I've had a train ride."

"I'll be having one, too, if I don't leave you now," Peter said with a grin as he turned to go.

Outside on the platform he called to them again.

"Give our regards to *Crime and the Criminal,*" Judy called back. "Good luck, Peter!"

"Keep the good luck for yourself!" he advised as the train started to move. "You'll need it."

And, with that rather ominous warning, they left him standing on the station platform. Miss Leonard turned to Judy after a moment and asked what he meant.

"Nothing," Judy answered dully. "He just doesn't like to have me go to this lecture without him."

"What sort of a lecture is it, Judy? We aren't really in any danger, are we?"

"Well, I should think," Judy replied guardedly, "that since Dad recommended it we ought to feel fairly safe. The lecturer is a noted physician. Dad has read some of his articles in medical magazines and thinks we'll be interested in hearing him.''

"Oh, that's all right, then," the music teacher said in evident relief. "I thought for a minute you might be keeping something from me."

Judy turned her face toward the window. She hadn't meant to deceive Miss Leonard. She wished she understood her father's reasons for wanting her to attend the lecture a little better. As it was, she had to admit it, she was actually afraid.

"This is going to be a lovely trip," Miss Leonard remarked as the train sped out into the open country.

Hillsides were so green they looked almost unreal. The snow that had covered the ground only a few days before was now melting from the sunny slopes. Only the woods still kept their white carpet.

"Shall we lunch in the dining car or wait until we reach Westlake?" asked Judy.

"I'd rather wait. It isn't a long trip and I'm not very hungry."

"I'm not either," Judy replied truthfully.

She felt so uneasy she doubted if she would be able to swallow a mouthful. The two men across the aisle kept glancing at her and this only added to her discomfort. But Miss Leonard appeared to be enjoying the trip.

"I mustn't spoil it for her," thought Judy. "It will be bad enough when we get there. Oh, I wonder why Dad wants me to take her. And the worst of it is, he wants her to be hypnotized."

"Judy, you're very quiet. Don't you feel well?" Miss Leonard asked after an hour or so of traveling.

"I'm not used to riding on trains. I'll feel better when we get there," Judy replied.

"Buy a new hat," advised Miss Leonard. "There's nothing like a new hat to give one a lift. Why, I can almost forget about my voice on a day like this with a spring hat on my head. Your father was certainly right about my needing a vacation."

In Westlake even Judy caught the contagious spring fever. The town itself was beautiful. The college buildings were built around a triangle of green with a deep pool in the center. Judy and Miss Leonard stood listening to the bell from the chapel tower and watching the goldfish that streaked through the quiet water of the pool.

"Here's where some of the students get a ducking occasionally, I imagine," remarked Miss Leonard. "And beyond is the lecture hall. Shall we stroll over and read the notices?"

"Later," said Judy. "Just now I'm hungry and there's a restaurant across the campus. It looks cozy. Let's eat."

Miss Leonard readily agreed and they entered

the restaurant which was called the College Grill. They seated themselves at a table for four near the center as all the small tables were taken.

"I said I was hungry," Judy thought as she scanned the menu, "and so I suppose I'll have to order something filling."

Baked bluefish, liver with onions . . . Ugh! None of them looked appetizing. But down at the bottom of the list Judy found her favorite dish, chicken croquettes with sweet potatoes and green peas.

"I'll have the croquettes with the fruit cup first and strawberry shortcake for dessert," she announced triumphantly.

"Judy! You are splurging. Well, then," Miss Leonard told the waiter, "I'll take the shrimp cocktail and steak and French fried potatoes with ice cream and coffee afterwards. Aren't we treating ourselves, though?" she added beaming at Judy. "I don't know when I've enjoyed anything so much."

Her eyes were shining under the perky hat. She looked lovely. She looked absolutely radiant. Judy's own eyes glowed with pleasure. Even if it couldn't last, she was glad she had given Linda this much pleasure.

At that moment the door of the restaurant opened and a group of laughing college girls came in. They made their way toward a table which had just been vacated. Judy glanced at them and, to her surprise, saw that one of them wore a light tan coat and had auburn hair exactly the shade of her own.

"Could she be my cousin Anna?" she thought excitedly. "Could she?"

The girl turned. Yes, she was like Judy.

"Anna, do sit with us," Judy begged, touching her hand.

"My glory!" exclaimed the girl whirling around. "Now I look like Anna. Who will it be next?"

"Why? Do you look like somebody else?" asked Judy quietly, concealing her inner excitement.

"You!" gasped the girl. "Why, I—I look like you. And a while back some stranger told me I looked like a girl named Judy. I went in to buy a cactus plant for my Japanese garden and the florist actually mistook me for her. I'm beginning to think I must be quintuplets." She studied Judy more closely. "But we're not quite alike. Your eyes are gray."

"They do look blue sometimes, I'm told," Judy replied, smiling. "And I wouldn't worry about being quintuplets if I were you. I'm the girl named Judy. Judy Bolton. And if you aren't Anna, then who are you?"

"I'm Roxy Zoller. And I will sit down since you invited me. There isn't room for me at that other table, anyway. I came in with some of the students. You're not one of them, are you?''

''No. Miss Leonard and I came in to hear the
lecture. It seems to me the lecturer's name was
Zoller,'' Judy added.

''Of course. I'm his daughter,'' the girl replied
proudly. ''I'm not one of the students, either, although Dad has spoken of sending me here next
year.''

''Isn't this a coincidence?'' exclaimed Miss
Leonard, still radiant, ''I've been trying to find
out what this lecture is all about, but Judy prefers
to keep me in the dark. Perhaps you can tell me.''

Judy took a deep breath and gripped the sides
of her chair. Now what was coming?

''I'll be delighted,'' Roxy replied. ''People do
get such strange first impressions of Dad's lectures. They come to them thinking they are going
to witness some sort of magic when, in reality,
they are quite scientific. Dad is a physician, you
know. He will probably tell you about some of
his cases tonight at the lecture—but of course that
isn't the exciting part. People really come hoping to be hypnotized——''

Miss Leonard gave a start and Judy could feel
her own face growing pale.

''Hoping to be—*what?*'' gasped the music
teacher.

CHAPTER XV

Roxy Explains

"Perhaps I shouldn't have used a word that has been so misued," Roxy apologized. "Dad prefers to call it the power of suggestion. It's working on the subconscious and he believes that the subconscious mind has wonderful, undiscovered healing powers. He has reason to believe it, too," she declared. "His most successful experiments have been with amnesia victims."

"Dad had one such patient," Judy put in quickly, hoping to divert Miss Leonard's mind from the main subject of the discussion. "He called in Dr. Faulkner, a brain specialist from New York. I met his daughter, Pauline. It seems I'm meeting the daughters of a great many famous doctors."

"Why, I know Pauline!" Roxy exclaimed. "I know her well. I've even met that funny old literary agent she works for. I thought it queer for a girl like Pauline to be working until I found out how fascinating her work is. I've used her as an example, trying to talk Dad out of sending me to college."

"But I should think you would want to go."

"And leave Dad? The old dear! Well, I'm onto his scheme to get rid of me. Besides, since Mother died, I can't help feeling that the younger children need someone besides a housekeeper."

"When did your mother die?" asked Judy, already abandoning the hope that Roxy might be her cousin.

"A year ago," the girl replied. "We all miss her terribly. I suppose you have both your parents."

"I can sympathize," Miss Leonard said gently. "I have no family at all."

"You're worse off than we are then. There are five of us, even without Mother. I'm the oldest and next comes Helen. She's fourteen. Then there's Margie, twelve and Terry, the youngest. He's going on ten and the principal reason why I refuse to leave home and go to college. We're all touring the country with Dad and he says it's part of our education. But this is his last lecture. I'll be half sorry when it's over and he's back in the hospital."

"What hospital?" asked Judy.

"Didn't you know? He's head of the phychopathic division of the Cleveland General Hospital. That's where we live."

"Oh, and this is just a tour—a lecture tour?"

Roxy nodded, apparently pleased that Judy was so interested.

"I'm finding out something, anyway," Judy

thought as she speared a piece of her croquette, "even if it is no more than the fact that my other theory was all wrong." This girl couldn't be her cousin, but it was still possible that she was the girl who should have received the black patent leather pocketbook.

"You're attending the lecture tonight?" she asked cautiously.

"Dad's lecture? Of course. I never miss them."

"Then your friends know just about where to find you on lecture nights, don't they?"

"Why, yes," Roxy replied, puzzled. "I never thought of that. But I guess they do. You're a funny girl. You ask so many questions."

"I have a reason," Judy said, deciding she might as well tell her. "I was mistaken for you too and someone gave me your pocketbook."

"That couldn't be," objected Roxy. "I haven't lost a pocketbook."

"But this was a new one. It had a note in it from Blackie——"

"Blackie?" Roxy questioned and Judy, glancing at her, thought for a minute that she saw fear in her eyes.

"Do you know him?" Miss Leonard asked, her voice sounding a little shocked.

"No. No, of course I don't." But Roxy lowered her eyes as she spoke and her face became flushed.

Judy gazed at her steadily.

"Well, since you don't know him, I suppose there's no reason for telling you what was in the note. There wouldn't be any information that you'd want badly enough to pay five hundred dollars——"

"Information? Five hundred dollars? Glory, no! Why, that much money would pay my tuition to college where I'd get all the information I wanted—and I don't want any! But what made you say that?"

"Well," Judy answered, "the note said that Blackie had some information that might be worth a fortune and then instructed someone to meet him after the lecture and have five hundred dollars. I wasn't going to any lecture and so I knew it couldn't mean me."

"But you're going to Dad's lecture——"

"I know I am—now. Can't you see, Roxy? I came here on purpose to find out about this message and deliver it if possible. Besides, I was afraid you might be in trouble."

Roxy shook her head in bewilderment.

"But you didn't know I existed."

"You only make it more confusing, Judy dear," Miss Leonard told her. "Why don't you finish your dinner before it grows cold, and explain the whole thing from the beginning?"

"That won't be necessary. I think I understand the note now," Roxy said in a low voice.

"It was meant for me at that. Blackie must be Mother's insurance agent. She probably borrowed that much money on her life insurance. I never thought of it before, but we haven't collected it. At least, I don't *think* we have. Dad never spoke of it and I'd forgotten all about it until this minute. Maybe Blackie took care of the premium himself and is going to collect the full amount if we pay the debt."

"No doubt that's what he wanted you to think," said Judy grimly. "But before you meet him, and before you pay him a single cent, I think you ought to know that the United States government wants him for blackmail."

The girl stared at Judy. Her blue eyes opened very wide and a little gasp came from her lips.

"No!" she protested. "No!"

"Be thankful that you've been told in time," Miss Leonard said with surprising calm for Judy knew that the thought of Blackie being at the lecture she planned to attend must be alarming to her as well as to Roxy.

"I had to tell you," Judy explained. "That's what I meant about thinking you might be in trouble."

"I guess I am," Roxy murmured. "Thanks. Thanks awfully." She took a swallow of water and then went on. "But Dad won't have to know, will he? He won't have to worry. He has to have his mind free for his lecture."

"I see no need of telling him," said Judy slicing her shortcake in half. "Please," she begged, "won't somebody help me out on this? It's a shame to waste it."

"I'm afraid you've taken my appetite away," Roxy laughed nervously.

"I've spoiled my own a little. But let's eat it as a duty," said Judy as she transferred half of the shortcake to a clean plate. "Want some, Linda?"

"No, thanks. The ice cream is all I can manage. Besides," Miss Leonard added, "I rather enjoy watching two girls who are so much alike eating the same thing."

"I guess we are alike at that," Roxy admitted, "if Blackie couldn't tell us apart. But I forgot to ask you about this girl, Anna. Who did you think I was when you first called me that?"

"Oh," said Judy as though it didn't matter much, "I have a cousin Anna or maybe it's Polly-anna or Susanna, I don't know. But I've never met her and I imagined she might look like me."

"I see. And you thought I might be your cousin?"

"Something like that. I had a lot of ideas in the back of my head. My cousin would be about your age. Her mother's name was Lucy Smeed."

"Well, my mother's name was Edith Terry and I know all my relatives—second, third and even some of my fourth cousins on both sides of the

family—and there's not a Smeed among them.
I can assure you, I haven't any cousin I've never
met.''

"You see," Miss Leonard said to Judy, "Roxy
can't be related to you. The resemblance is just
coincidence.''

"I suppose it is," Judy admitted, "but I would
like to find my cousin.''

"We can be friends even if we can't be cousins," Roxy reassured her as she pushed back her
chair. "I have a whole afternoon to kill and perhaps you and Linda—shall I call you Linda?''

"Yes, do," urged Miss Leonard. "I'm a
teacher—or was," she corrected herself, her face
clouding at the thought, "and I heard 'Miss'
enough in the classroom.''

"What did you teach?" asked Roxy with interest.

"Music," Miss Leonard said briefly.

"Then you must be fond of concerts. I'm not,
but I have a ticket to one this afternoon and if
you'd care to use it . . .'' she hesitated. "But I
don't suppose you'd want to go alone.''

"I wouldn't mind. What do you think, Judy?''

"I think it's a splendid idea," she declared enthusiastically.

There was something more she wanted to say to
Roxy and she couldn't very well say it in the
presence of Miss Leonard.

CHAPTER XVI

A Dangerous Plan

"Do you really think she will enjoy it all alone?" Roxy asked anxiously as Miss Leonard entered the concert hall.

"Of course she will. She loves music. Besides," Judy confided, "I couldn't tell you before, but she was a beautiful singer. Something happened to her voice and Dad has an idea that being hypnotized will help her. I'm sure I don't see how but perhaps your father can arrange to let her be one of his subjects——"

"I'm sure he can," Roxy replied. "I'll tell him about her."

Would it be as simple as all that? Judy had not quite lost her fear of the hypnotist. Even though she had been reassured by his lovely daughter that hypnotism was scientific and did effect wonderful cures, it was still terrifying to her. It might be all right for Miss Leonard but not for Judy. Tonight, of all nights, she must be able to think clearly and swiftly. She must not be under the direction of anyone except herself.

The two girls were walking down College Avenue, the main street in Westlake, when Roxy suddenly stopped and clutched Judy's arm.

"Don't look, but I believe we're being followed," she said in a low voice.

Footsteps sounded clearly behind them but Judy, glancing back, could see no one.

"I told you not to look. He hides the minute we turn around and—and I think it's Blackie," she added in a whisper.

"Let's just walk casually into this hat store," Judy suggested. "I wanted to buy a hat anyway." But to herself she was thinking that if their follower did turn out to be Blackie she could easily call the police from the telephone inside.

From behind a door curtain they could peer out without being seen, but Roxy had only a fleeting glimpse of the man who had been walking behind them while Judy missed seeing him altogether.

"Was it Blackie?" she asked as Roxy stepped back from the door.

"I don't think so. But we can look again later. I believe he's waiting inside the entrance next door."

"But why would anyone want to follow us?" asked Judy in a puzzled voice.

"I don't know," Roxy replied. "I'm afraid to think. I almost wish you hadn't told me anything about Blackie. Everything's so mixed up now. I keep wondering about Mother——"

"What about her?" asked Judy eagerly.

"Why she was so friendly with him—and why

he never came except when Dad was away. She seemed a little bit afraid of him too. She always watched him so carefully and was so especially polite and afterwards she always warned us not to say anything about his visit. But of course it was all right," Roxy added. "Mother was a jewel. We all loved her dearly."

"What was she like?" questioned Judy, still clinging to the hope that, somehow, Roxy's mother might be Lucy.

"Black hair, brown eyes," Roxy described her. "Terry is the only one of us children who has Mother's eyes. The rest of us all have blue eyes like Dad's, but Helen has Mother's jet black hair."

Jet black? And Lucy's hair was light brown, so Miss Leonard said. She had died, not one but seventeen years before, and Judy's grandparents had attended the funeral. She couldn't have had a whole family of children. There was no use thinking about it any more, Judy decided, and turned her attention to hats.

"Let's try on some of the spring models," she suggested. "Miss Leonard says there's nothing like a new hat to lift up a person's spirit."

"Mine needs lifting," Roxy declared, seating herself at one of the tables before a large mirror.

Judy sat down beside her and the two girls studied their reflections.

"I guess we aren't so much alike as I thought at

first," Judy said thoughtfully. "Your eyes are as blue as the sky."

"Yours are more like the sky on a cloudy day when the sun is trying to shine through," Roxy observed poetically.

"Your eyebrows are nicer. I've often thought I should pluck mine."

"Don't," Roxy advised. "Those thin pencilled line eyebrows make you look so unnatural."

But Judy was interested in hair. "Did anyone else in your family have hair like yours?"

"Red? Glory, no! Redheads are sometimes freaks. Didn't you know that?"

"Freaks? What do you mean by that, Roxy?"

"Well," she explained, "I mean that once in a blue moon you'll see a red-haired child in a family where everyone else has ordinary colored hair. I'll bet you don't have any redheaded brothers and sisters, either."

"No," Judy admitted. "I have only one brother and his hair is light brown."

"It's the same way with us," Roxy continued, "I'm different from my brother and sisters because I'm a redhead, but we all look alike across the eyes. Our noses are the same too—all narrow and perfectly straight. Yours turns up a little at the end."

Judy giggled at that.

"It really does worry you that we look so much alike, doesn't it?" she asked. "As for me, I'm flattered. I never knew how attractive I was before."

The saleswoman who had been hovering around them now spoke.

"So you aren't twins after all. I thought you might want to buy two hats just alike."

"We do," Judy assured her, a plan beginning to shape itself in her mind. "Something with veils that just cover our noses. You see?" She turned to Roxy who was still studying the mirror. "We look more alike when you can't see the upper part of our faces."

"That's right. But what are you planning?" Roxy asked suspiciously.

"A disguise to fool Blackie. That is, if you'll allow me to meet him after the lecture tonight."

"You mean in my place?" gasped Roxy. "But that might be dangerous."

"I don't think so," Judy replied lightly. "Most of the things you're afraid of aren't so terrible when you stand up and face them. I'm sure you'll think it's silly, but I'm rather afraid to meet your father. However, I'm going to take the bull by the horns and meet him anyway."

"But why should you be afraid to meet Dad?" asked Roxy in surprise.

"It's because of my mother mostly," Judy confessed as she tilted the little hat with the veil at a different angle and discovered that it made her look still more like Roxy.

"There we are. Tweedledum and Tweedledee," she announced triumphantly.

Roxy frowned at the two reflections.

"I'm not at all sure that I like being one of twins," she remarked. "Wouldn't it be awful if we were both adopted and our mothers and fathers weren't really our mothers and fathers at all?"

"You're not adopted, are you?" Judy asked, unable to rid herself of that first triumphant feeling that she had found her cousin.

"Of course I'm not," Roxy replied impatiently. "I just said it would be awful if I were. I know very well I never had a twin or an unknown cousin or any other such mysterious things. It's your family that's mysterious. What do you mean about being afraid of Dad because of your mother?"

"Well, she thinks hypnotists are apt to make you do things that you wouldn't do ordinarily," Judy attempted to explain. "I mean, they control your will and so, naturally, they control your actions."

"I suppose, in a way, they do," Roxy admitted. "But Dad isn't like some. He'd never make a subject do anything ridiculous or—or perhaps I should say anything that he'd be ashamed of. And he always takes you out of it before the evening is over."

"Takes you out of *what*, Roxy?"

"The spell," she said. "But wait, you'll see when he puts you under."

"But Miss Leonard is going to be his subject. He won't hypnotize *me*, will he?" asked Judy in alarm.

"Why, naturally," Roxy replied. "He hypnotizes his entire audience."

"But he mustn't—not if I'm going to see Blackie."

"What does that have to do with it?"

"I must be able to think!" cried Judy. "There are so many things I haven't yet figured out."

"You'll think all the more clearly after the lecture," Roxy prophesied.

It was useless to discuss the matter further, Judy could see. The girl had unbounded faith in her father's profession. But to Judy hypnotism was still puzzling and—yes, she had to admit it, a little frightening as well.

"Pardon me, but is the gentleman outside waiting for you?" the saleswoman asked as she accepted two bills in payment for the two hats that Judy and Roxy had selected.

They glanced at each other apprehensively.

"I wouldn't have asked you," the woman went on, "but he keeps peering in at the window and, to tell you the truth, he's making me a little nervous."

"If he's making you nervous, what do you think he's making us?" Judy replied thoughtlessly. "We came in here principally because we thought he was following us."

"You don't say! Well, I don't want to hurry you——"

But the girls were gone before she could finish speaking.

Judy thought she would surprise Blackie and peek around the corner at him before he could fall in behind her again. But, instead, she surprised herself. The waiting man did not fit Blackie's description at all. But she had seen him before. He was one of the two men who had sat across from her on the train.

"Know him?" she whispered to Roxy.

"I never saw him before in my life," the girl replied.

"He looks very respectable. I don't believe he's very dangerous. Let's go," Judy urged, taking Roxy's arm as they stepped out of the doorway.

The hypnotist's daughter pulled back. "Do you think it is safe for us to separate?"

"Yes," Judy replied confidently. "I am sure the man won't follow us." Then she turned toward the hotel but not without first reminding Roxy that she would see her again at the lecture.

"If I go," Roxy replied. But Judy guessed, from the tone of her voice that she wouldn't be there. The man, she saw, had given up following either of them and was now buying a ticket to a newsreel theatre across the street.

"It's too bad he isn't Blackie," Judy said to herself regretfully. "I'd know right where to find him for the next hour and the police could easily arrest him."

Blackie, she imagined, would not be that easy to catch.

CHAPTER XVII

The Power of Suggestion

"Roxy Zoller is certainly one of the most puzzling people I have ever come across," Judy declared that evening when she and Miss Leonard were in their hotel room dressing for the lecture.

"How do you mean?" asked the music teacher. "She seemed to me to be quite as honest and straightforward as anyone would expect under the circumstances. Altogether quite a charming girl."

"I thought so too," Judy agreed, "and yet there's something—I don't know just what—that puzzles me. I can't get away from the feeling that she is my cousin, and yet, the more I talk with her, the more positive proof she offers that she isn't. She even looks like her brother and sisters, she says, across the eyes."

"I see you've hidden your own eyes quite successfully under the veil of that new hat," Miss Leonard observed with a smile.

"They're gray," Judy said, "and Roxy's are blue. That means that mine must be blue for the evening. I expect Blackie to give whatever information he has to me. It's the only way I'll ever find out the truth."

141

"You mean—Oh, Judy! You're not going to meet him? Please take my advice and don't do anything as rash as all that."

"If anything happens," Judy told her calmly, "you have Mr. Trent's number and also the number of the local police. Now let's just forget it and enjoy the lecture. I'm rather anxious to meet Roxy's family and see just how much she does resemble them."

All Miss Leonard's protests could not change Judy's plans. Eight o'clock found them in the crowd of people that pushed their way into the auditorium. From remarks that Judy chanced to overhear on her way in she judged that most of those who were attending the lecture knew as little about hypnotism as she did. Miss Leonard grew increasingly nervous.

"Did you see that poster outside?" she asked. "It says that subjects will be chosen from the audience. Does that mean some of us may be hypnotized?"

"I hope so," Judy replied, determined to accomplish her purpose. "Don't you think it would be fun to try it?"

"I'm not sure." Miss Leonard's tone was thoughtful. "Once I might have agreed to it. Lucy and I planned to hear a hypnotist once, but we were forbidden to go. It wasn't a lecture like this, given by a prominent man. The act was put on in a side show at the circus. It makes me shudder to think of what might have happened——''

''But you didn't go?''

''No. Oh, no! Neither my parents nor Lucy's would hear of it. This brings it all back, exactly the way she stormed at them and told them they weren't fair.''

''It would be queer, wouldn't it, if this man turned out to be the same hypnotist?''

''There'd be no way of telling. I never saw the other man. I don't even remember his name.''

''I wish you did,'' Judy remarked wistfully as they found their seats.

Fortunately, they were early enough to secure seats near the front of the auditorium, so that the platform where the speaker would stand was directly in front of them.

''Here he comes now!'' they heard an excited whisper.

Judy looked about her but saw no one who looked in the least as she had imagined Dr. Zoller would look. She could not find Roxy in the crowd either but, as she turned to look for her, an animated young girl with black hair and blue eyes rushed up and seized her hand.

''I knew you'd come, Roxy Zoller! What was the idea of fooling us and saying you wouldn't?'' she began excitedly.

Judy pulled back her veil, looking steadily at the girl. Her eyes were blue and their wide, sur-

prised expression told Judy that this must be
Roxy's sister Helen.

"Why, you're—you're not Roxy. I beg your
pardon," the girl stammered, "but my sister has
a hat exactly like yours and her hair is the same
color——"

"I know," Judy interrupted, "I met her this
afternoon and I'm taking her place tonight. She's
supposed to meet somebody and I'm meeting him
instead."

"Oh, I get it. You made up to look like her."
And Helen giggled.

"Let me meet the rest of the family before your
father begins to talk," Judy suggested. Then she
introduced herself and Miss Leonard and in another moment they had met the younger Zollers.
Margie resembled Roxy even more than Helen did.
The boy, too, except for his brown eyes, was like
the rest of the family. They all said that they had
teased and coaxed but still Roxy had refused to
come with them.

"I knew it must be boy trouble," young Terry
declared. "Girls make me sick, always mooning
over somebody and spoiling their own good times.
But you'll fool this one all right. Quick! Pull
down your veil and Dad will think you're Roxy
too."

A middle-aged man of medium height with
slightly graying hair was coming rapidly down
the aisle. Now he stopped, patting Terry's head

and saying in a kindly voice, "Too late to fool your old Dad, Son. Roxy has already told me about her friend." He clasped Judy's hand and then turned to Miss Leonard. "She has told me about you, too. Did you enjoy the concert?"

"Very much indeed," the music teacher replied. "It was kind of her to give me the ticket."

"She was glad to do it. Now back to your seats, youngsters," he said to the children. "Remember, you're to sit quietly and pay attention——"

But someone had recognized him and a burst of applause drowned out the rest of what he was trying to tell them. Judy, Miss Leonard and the children, now back in their own seats, joined in the hand-clapping as Dr. Zoller stepped up on the platform.

"Friends," he began, "I suppose you are disappointed. Here I am an ordinary little man in an ordinary gray business suit and yet I have the presumption to pose as a hypnotist. Certainly you imagined me as an altogether different person. I should have flaming eyes, sweeping black robes, perhaps a wand——"

Here the audience interrupted with laughter as he stretched his hand to indicate the imaginary wand of which he spoke.

As he continued his talk Judy began to understand the persuasive power of his voice. It was true. He did appear to be an ordinary man, but no other speaker had ever kept and held her attention as he did. That holding of a person's attention, he explained, was hypnotism.

"We have all been hypnotized," he went on, his voice becoming more vibrant, "by books, by advertising, by a stirring address, by the radio. Who among us has not bought a certain tooth paste because four out of every five have some dread gum disease, or bathed with some particular soap because even our best friends won't tell us? That's hypnotism, friends. But tonight I am not selling you anything. I am only trying to tell you that this great power of suggestion may be used or misused, may become a force either for good or for evil.

"Suppose you say to yourself when you arise in the morning, 'I'm still tired. I ache all over. I can't possibly get any work done today.' Isn't it reasonable to suppose that the day will see little accomplished?

"But, on the other hand, suppose you say, 'This is a glorious day. I feel fine. I feel wonderful. I'm glad to be alive——"

"Aren't you?" Miss Leonard whispered to Judy, her face still fixed on the speaker, listening to every word.

Judy nodded. She did feel lifted up. But was this all there was to hypnotism? Was it simply listening to a talk?

"And now comes the part of the program for which you have all been waiting," Dr. Zoller an-

nounced after another five minutes of explanation.
"Now I shall actually demonstrate how a person
can be hypnotized. But first remember this! The
subject must be willing. I have no power except
the power you give me. Your mind must be ready
to receive whatever I suggest. Now!"

The audience stirred as though it were one
great body. One could have heard a pin drop.
Then it seemed that everyone began whispering at
once. "You do it! You! You!"

Judy nudged Miss Leonard. "Why don't you
go up?"

"No, you!" she whispered back.

"Just as I thought," Dr. Zoller announced.
"No one will try it. Suppose, then, that you all
concentrate on what I am saying. I think, by the
end of five minutes, at least ten of you will be glad
to come forward. Now do exactly as I tell you.
Keep your eyes fixed on me, your hands clasped
together. Now clasp your hands tighter—tighter
—tighter——"

Both Judy and Miss Leonard were following his
words carefully. They seemed unable to do anything else.

"Clasp your hands tighter—tighter—" he kept
repeating.

Judy's knuckles were beginning to show white.
The ends of her fingers were as red as blood. But
still she felt compelled to clasp her hands more
tightly together.

"Now," announced the doctor with a gleam of triumph in his eyes, "your hands are locked together. You cannot get them apart!"

"It's true!" gasped Miss Leonard, struggling to break apart her locked fingers.

"Mine, too," agreed Judy too filled with the wonder of what had happened to think of how utterly helpless she was without the use of her hands. "They're locked!" she exclaimed as though pleased with the amazing power of the hypnotist's suggestion. Again she fixed her eyes upon the speaker waiting, not for her own will to unclasp her hands, but for his voice to direct her.

"That's enough," he said, "I think now that quite a number of you will come forward. Raise your locked hands above your heads—slowly—slowly. Now you are getting up. Now you are walking down the aisle. Now you are nearing the platform."

His voice was magnetic. More than a dozen people joined the procession, ghostlike, moving as in pantomime, coming slowly forward. Judy felt her feet moving, felt her clasped hands on her head and knew she was among them.

CHAPTER XVIII

Under the Spell

It was not until she turned to face the audience that Judy realized how deeply she had been concentrating her attention on the hypnotist, allowing him to direct her thoughts as well as her actions. It was not until then that she sensed the danger of the situation in which she now found herself.

"You are going to sleep," the doctor was telling her over and over in a hypnotic monotone. "Sit down in the chair. There. Now you are comfortable. Everything is quiet and you are going to sleep."

He passed his hands before her eyes with a dreamlike movement and repeated, "Sleep. Sleep. Now you are closing your eyes. Now you are sound asleep."

Tearing her attention away from him, Judy forced herself to the conclusion that she could not really be asleep. If she were, then how could she hear what he was saying? And suddenly she knew that she must not be asleep. She had things to do.

"Sleep. Sleep," he was still repeating.

"But I'm not asleep!"

Judy's voice rang as clear as a bell. A little ripple of excitement spread over the audience but it soon died away.

"This," explained Dr. Zoller in a voice as undisturbed as though nothing had happened, "is what often occurs when the subject is afraid. But you are not afraid any more," he said, turning to Judy whose attention was drawn to him once more. "Nothing can frighten you now. Nothing can frighten you. Unclasp your hands and return to your seat. Have no fear. You will not be hypnotized again."

"No?" questioned Judy, rising from her chair as though she were in a slow-motion picture, half-reluctant to leave the platform.

"Unclasp your hands. Return to your seat," he repeated in a peculiarly persuasive voice. "You are not afraid any more. Nothing can frighten you. Now you are going back to your seat laughing and happy."

"Of course," Judy said to some stranger she passed on her way to her seat, "it was silly to be afraid, wasn't it?"

She laughed aloud and, for a moment, she couldn't understand the queer look the stranger gave her. She had done exactly what the hypnotist had told her she would do.

"But," she thought to herself as she watched the others still on the platform, "I won't be hypnotized again. Nothing can frighten me. I guess it won't be so bad meeting Blackie if I'm not afraid.''

It was some time before Judy noticed the same man who had been following her during the afternoon sitting just two seats behind her. She wondered vaguely why he was there. But she was not disturbed by his presence as the four words, ''Nothing can frighten me'' kept repeating themselves over and over in her brain.

Dr. Zoller had said she would not be hypnotized again but Judy was curiously glad that she had been. Now she knew how it felt. She could understand how the stranger who had now taken her place in the chair was being directed. She had surrendered her will completely to the will of the hypnotist. He had now taken her out of the first trancelike sleep and her eyes were wide open watching him as he pretended to cut a slice of cherry pie for her to eat.

In reality the cherry pie was a folded piece of paper. The audience gasped as she took a large bite of it and assured the doctor that it was very good pie.

''The crust is a little tough though,'' she added as she swallowed the paper.

One by one the others on the platform were hypnotized and then ''taken out of it'' as Roxy had expressed it. They returned to their seats each having been given some helpful suggestion such as Judy's ''Nothing can frighten you.''

The woman who ate the imaginary pie was told she would not worry any more. A man was told he would make gardening his hobby. A pale young girl was told how much better her health would be.

"I feel better already," she replied as she took her seat.

Her eyes did look brighter and there was new color in her cheeks. What magic there seemed to be in Dr. Zoller's suggestions! As Miss Leonard finally took the chair before him, Judy almost held her breath, listening.

"Unclasp your hands, my dear. It was not necessary for you to keep them locked together so tightly. Now stretch your fingers. Relax them. Stretch them again. Now you are stretching them upward—upward. You are reaching for something. What is it you are trying to touch?" asked the doctor as Linda's fingers stretched wide and she raised her arms toward the ceiling.

"The stars," she whispered almost inaudibly. "I'm reaching for the stars."

Someone in the audience laughed.

"You hear nothing except my voice. There is no other sound in the room," the hypnotist assured her. "The audience has all gone home. You and I are alone here and we know each other very well. We trust each other. We are both reaching for the stars. But what will you do with the stars when you get them, Linda?"

"Linda?" she questioned. "You know my name?"

"I know all about you, my dear, but what will you do with the stars?"

"I think I'll make wreaths of them. Little circles of white stars on a blue sky." And she formed her hands in the shape of a circle.

"It's the subconscious that's speaking," Dr. Zoller informed his audience, now watching intently. "Stars," he continued persuasively, "like those on the dress you are wearing?"

Miss Leonard's dress was a flowered print, rose on black, but she must have imagined it as he described it for she glanced down, smoothed the material and said, "Yes, that's it. I have it on now. Lucy's mother made it for my birthday. I was just sixteen."

"You are still sixteen. You are still wearing the dress. You are going to sing in the church choir——"

Judy's eyes widened and she leaned forward in her seat unable to believe what she had heard. Dr. Zoller must be a mind reader as well as a hypnotist, for surely he had no way of knowing that Miss Leonard had worn a blue dress with circles of white stars in it on the night she first sang in the choir.

"You are going to sing," he repeated. "You are going to sing a hymn. Now you are in the church. Now you are standing in the choir loft waiting for the music. Now you hear the music. Now you begin.''

Miss Leonard hesitated. "Is it *Lead Kindly Light?* But no!" she cried covering her face with her hands. "I can't sing that. I've lost my voice and I shall never sing again."

"Ah, but that wasn't when you were sixteen. You're sixteen now," Dr. Zoller reminded her patiently. "You're going to sing something about stars because there are stars in your dress. Don't you see them, Linda?"

"Here?" she questioned, pointing to one of the rose-colored flowers on her black dress. "Yes, I see them."

"And you're going to sing?"

"Yes," she repeated dreamily, "I'm going to sing."

Then, to everybody's amazement, she stepped to the center of the platform and began humming, first softly, then clearly and distinctly. She seemed to gain confidence in herself as she went on and finally the words came, clear and sweet:

"Will there be any stars, any stars in my crown
When at evening the sun goeth down . . .''

As Judy listened, she thought she had never heard anyone sing more beautifully. But the audience was warned not to clap when she was finished. They were in church, the hypnotist reminded them.

"We do not usually go to sleep in church," he added, "but now Linda is going back to sleep. Our subject's name is Linda Leonard and she thought she had lost her voice. But when she wakes up she will have no fear. She will always be able to sing."

"Always," Miss Leonard agreed, closing her eyes and apparently falling asleep in her chair.

In a few words, Dr. Zoller explained the miracle. By reaching the subconscious mind he had cured Miss Leonard of a fear she had not known was there—the fear that she had lost her voice. What had caused the fear he was unable to tell. Perhaps, at some time or another, she had been especially anxious to sing . . .

"At Grandma's funeral," Judy thought.

"Or perhaps," he continued, "music was connected with some past tragedy. But our subject has forgotten it now or, if she remembers it, the memory is no longer painful. Shall we have her sing for you again when she wakes up?"

"Yes! Yes!" came enthusiastic voices from the audience.

Judy was watching and listening so attentively that she did not notice Helen Zoller as she slipped into the seat beside her. She gave a start when the girl touched her arm.

"Did I frighten you?" she asked in a whisper.

"Gracious no," Judy whispered back. "Didn't you hear your father tell me that nothing could frighten me any more? I just didn't know you were there and—and, well, you did startle me."

Helen laughed. "He does that to everybody, makes 'em feel ready to conquer the world. I came over to tell you that Roxy's here," she added in a lower voice.

"She is? Where?" asked Judy excitedly.

"Outside. She won't come in and she doesn't know I saw her. But she's there. I thought you'd like to know."

"Thanks, Helen. I'm going out for a minute," Judy decided. "Will you tell Miss Leonard I'll be right back? I mean, when she comes out of this—this trance she's in. She doesn't know I exist right now. But will you please tell her I'm all right and that she mustn't worry?"

"Gladly," Helen replied, watching Judy as she slipped out of the auditorium.

The man two seats behind her also watched her and she saw him leave his seat and walk over where he could still see her from the window.

Outside she found Roxy hidden in the shadows cast by one of the great spruce trees in front of the building.

"There's a phone call for you, Roxy," Judy said, thinking quickly. "Inside, in the booth. It was a man's voice. Probably Blackie. He said, 'Get Roxy Zoller to the phone and if you can't find her tell her not to wait any longer——' "

"Thanks," breathed Roxy. "Whew! That's a relief. I'll see if he's still on the wire."

"If he isn't," Judy advised her, "you might as well go in and hear the rest of your father's lecture. It's *good*. You may be in time to hear Linda sing."

Roxy hurried inside the building and Judy took her place in the shadow of the spruce tree. There hadn't really been a telephone call. But Judy felt that the good she might accomplish excused the deception. It was apparent that Roxy had been waiting to meet Blackie and pay him the money he had demanded. For some reason that Judy could not understand, she was afraid not to pay him.

As for Judy herself, she was ready to dare anything in her present high spirits.

"Nothing can frighten me," she kept repeating over and over to herself as she waited.

Inside she could hear Miss Leonard singing again. Yes, she knew it, Roxy was in there listening. No one would leave the auditorium for at least half an hour.

Thinking of the man who had followed her, Judy pressed next to the tree so that she could not be seen from the window.

"Nothing can frighten me," she told herself still more determinedly as a car stopped in front of the building. A man stepped out and Judy recognized Blackie.

Hugging the thought closer and closer, for she knew she would have need of the new courage the hypnotist had given her, Judy stole noiselessly down the tree-shaded pathway.

"Here I am," she whispered, touching Blackie's coat sleeve. "The note said you wanted to see me."

CHAPTER XIX

A Ride in the Night

"Smart girl," said Blackie, whirling about so that he could look at Judy. "So you are interested in claiming your fortune? But we can't talk here."

"Where then?" asked Judy. But even the hypnotic four words could not still the furious pounding of her heart.

"In the car," he said briefly, taking her arm.

"No," she protested, drawing back in alarm. "You can say anything you have to say while we're walking."

"I said *in the car!*" And he fairly dragged her into the seat beside him. Before she could cry out, even if she had thought it wise, which she didn't, the car was purring noiselessly down the street.

"Now I am in a predicament," she thought. "But nothing can frighten me."

"What was that?" demanded Blackie.

Without realizing it, Judy had spoken her thoughts aloud.

"I said *nothing can frighten me,*" she replied in a clear voice.

"You've been listening to your father's lingo,"

growled Blackie, "but you may not be so proud of him, or your mother either, when you hear what I have to tell you."

"My glory! Is it that awful?" exclaimed Judy, borrowing Roxy's expression.

"Well, do you want to hear it? Did you bring the money?"

"How do I know the information you have to give me is worth five hundred dollars?" Judy asked calmly.

"You may take my word for it. I am thinking only of your welfare," he replied with exaggerated politeness.

"But what if I don't want to hear it?"

"Then you are refusing to hear the extent of your own fortune. Now if I were in your place, Roxanna Zoller——"

"Roxanna?" gasped Judy without thinking.

"What's the matter?" he demanded, immediately suspicious.

"Oh, nothing," she replied collecting her thoughts as well as she could and resuming the pose, "only most people call me Roxy. I didn't think you knew my whole name."

"That ain't all I know," declared Blackie, forgetting to be polite. "But first, where's the money?"

"I thought—I thought it was for Mother's insurance," stammered Judy, trying to say what she imagined Roxy would say. "I thought I could pay it tomorrow."

"You know I don't return to collect debts. You've heard me tell that much to your mother. And you know what that gun on the note means. It means I collect today—or else!"

"Oh!" said Judy. "Oh, glory!" she said again, attempting frantically to think. "Or else *what?*"

"Don't act as dumb as you look!" snapped Blackie, turning the car onto a wide country road.

"Nothing can frighten me," Judy whispered for reassurance. Aloud she asked, "Aren't you going a little bit out of the way?"

"That depends. I intend to go out of the way to get that five hundred," Blackie declared. "I need it bad. And I'll get it, too," he added threateningly. "If you didn't bring it then I know where you can find it and that's where we're headed for."

"Where?" she asked, controlling her voice as well as she could and hoping it sounded like Roxy's. In the dark with her face half concealed by the veil she felt sure Blackie would never know the difference from her appearance.

"To Cleveland. That's where," he answered gruffly. "You'll find five hundred and more, if I want it, in your father's safe."

"Oh! So that's your plan? You might as well give me the information on the way there," Judy said artfully, "since you're so sure of getting the money."

"Who said I was sure? But I've got another plan if this one don't work."

"Kidnapping, I suppose. But aren't you afraid of the G-men?"

"Huh! Those birds want me so bad they couldn't want me worse if I committed a murder. And believe me," Blackie added in an ominous voice, "it ain't always a wise policy to deliver a kidnap victim alive."

"Hypnotism makes a person hard to kill. Perhaps we can find some other way out of this mess," Judy suggested, her voice still calm.

"Say! You have been hypnotized at that," Blackie declared, turning his head to stare at Judy. "You wasn't an especially brave kid as I remember."

"Nothing can frighten me. Nothing can frighten me," Judy repeated in a trancelike voice.

As they sped along the unfamiliar road toward Cleveland, she could see that she was unnerving Blackie a little.

Her own courage amazed her, but still she clung fast to the four magic words. She did not let herself tremble at the thought of what would happen when they reached Cleveland and when she, who knew nothing about Dr. Zoller's home, tried to find her way about in it.

Instead, she cheered herself with the thought that already she had a clue. Roxy's name was Roxanna and it was . . . anna on the postal card. If she ever escaped from Blackie she might be able to figure out something from that. But how could Roxy be her cousin if she really belonged to the Zoller family? The resemblance she bore to her brother and sisters was certainly more than coincidence. Helen and Margie had eyes so exactly like Roxy's that at a glance anyone would know them to be sisters. Judy, suddenly conscious of her own eyes, felt her hat to make sure her veil was securely attached to it.

"Say, what's the idea of that veil you're wearing?" Blackie demanded, interpreting the motion.

"You wouldn't want either of us to be recognized, would you?"

"You're almost too clever," grunted Blackie as he fixed his eyes on the road ahead.

"It must be midnight, if not later," thought Judy. She had no idea how far they had traveled but before long she knew that they were close to the Ohio state line. She could see a lake—it would be Lake Erie—shimmering like silver in the light of the full moon that now rode high in the sky.

A thousand stars looked down to renew her faith in the beauty and tranquility she knew existed even in a world that had such characters as Blackie in it.

"Nothing can frighten me," she repeated sleepily as she let her head droop to one side and finally rest on her own shoulder. A cramp in her neck awakened her much later. Daylight was just streaking the sky.

"Where are we?" she asked sitting up, dazedly.

"You *were* sound asleep," Blackie snorted. "Don't you recognize your own home town?"

A street sign said Euclid Avenue, but it meant nothing to Judy who had never visited Cleveland before.

"I'm dizzy," she announced. "My eyes are misty. I can't see very well."

Blackie chuckled evilly.

"Maybe your doting papa carried his act a little too far and hypnotized his precious daughter out of her eyesight."

"I shall not mind being blind," said Judy in the trancelike voice she had assumed the night before. "I am not afraid. Nothing can frighten me."

"Don't start that again. Say!" Blackie peered at her more closely. "Your eyes do look different at that—sort of greenish——"

"They feel different," declared Judy. "I can hardly open them." And, deliberately, she closed her lids, for it was now full daylight and she knew she must keep her eyes hidden if she expected to continue posing as Roxy.

"Don't go to sleep again," Blackie warned her. "You'll have to point out the house."

"But I told you everything's blurred," Judy objected. "I can't see to tell one house from another."

"Curses!" he exclaimed in exact imitation of the villain in the funny papers.

"Foiled again?" she questioned innocently. "Or must you stop in a cigar store and look up the number?"

"And let you escape? That will hardly be necessary. There it is anyhow," he pointed out triumphantly. "Your father obliged us with a sign."

"A doctor would be rather dumb not to put up a sign, wouldn't he?" asked Judy lightly to keep up her spirits.

Blackie turned to her impatiently.

"Well, have you got the house key?"

"The house key? Oh, my glory! It's in my other pocketbook."

"You mean the one I gave you?"

"Yes. And do forgive me, Blackie," she added in honeyed tones, "I forgot to thank you for it."

"Get out of the car," he snarled. "You can thank me with cash. That's what talks. You'll have to wake the housekeeper if she ain't up already."

"Wake the housekeeper?" Judy repeated dazedly.

"Sure. Snap out of it! Mrs. Webber knows me as well as you do. She'll think I've come as a friend." He chuckled and added, "That's what you kids always used to think when I dropped in to see your mother."

"If you'll act like a friend it may help," Judy reminded him as he rang the bell.

CHAPTER XX

A Desperate Situation

AFTER several repeated rings a rather heavy woman with kind eyes still blinking from sleep opened the door and peered out through a crack. She blinked her eyes again and then opened the door wider.

"Is it Roxy or do my eyes deceive me?" she inquired. "Land sakes, child! I hardly knew you in that outlandish hat."

"I feel a little faint!" gasped Judy, stumbling and almost falling into the woman's arms. "Won't you help me to my room?"

"Wait a minute!" Blackie blocked the way with his foot. "We're going to your father's office first and you're going to pay me that insurance premium. Don't you remember?"

Judy sank on the stairs. Her dizziness was only partly pretended. But she mustn't give up. Somewhere she must find the courage to go on.

"Now look here, Mr. Black." Mrs. Webber, the housekeeper, became suddenly belligerent. "I've seen you wheedle money out of Mrs. Zoller claiming it was for insurance but never a cent of insurance money came into this house after she was dead. What's more, you're not going to touch a cent that belongs to her daughter—or to him either," the woman added, her eyes blazing. "And if the child's tired or faint, that's what I'm here for. And if she wants to be helped to her room——"

But, to Judy's horror, the woman's words were stopped by Blackie's hand which shot swiftly around from behind and held her mouth firmly shut.

"You can't do that!" screamed Judy as he whipped a handkerchief out of his pocket and proceeded to use it as a gag.

"Can't I though! There, Mrs. Webber," he announced as he pushed her into a closet, "you won't be bothering us for a while."

Judy could control herself no longer.

"You beast!" she cried. "You'll pay for this——"

"Now you're acting more like yourself," he interrupted triumphantly. "I thought that would bring you to your senses. Now shall we go to your father's office and get the money, or shall I take you along in the car as I promised? Your father would pay considerably more than five hundred dollars for your return."

"I—I can't see the office," she brought out slowly.

"That's good!" snorted Blackie. "I guess you are going blind. It's right beside you."

"Is it?" asked Judy, feeling for the door. The knob turned at her touch. "So it is!" she exclaimed in pretended amazement. "But now that we're here, what good will it do?"

"Plenty," Blackie replied, his hand on the pocket where Judy knew he kept his gun. "Now you're going to open the safe for me. You know the combination."

"I wish I did," Judy said, making her voice sound sad. "But I seem to have forgotten it. Couldn't you come back another time?"

"You know I couldn't! If you've forgotten the combination then call your father and find out what it is. I'll be standing right beside you," warned Blackie, "and if you say anything to spoil my plans, into the car you go! Get it?"

"I get it," replied Judy. She did, indeed, understand what a call to Roxy's father might mean. All this time she had been missing but if she called Dr. Zoller he would know it wasn't Roxy calling. He would know it was Judy. He would know where to find her.

"Tell him," Blackie directed, "that a friend of your mother's brought you home. Tell him you thought it would save him the expense of a return ticket and then explain that you're out of funds and would like to borrow some money out of his safe——"

"Will he agree to that?" asked Judy.

"He ain't in the habit of refusing you anything, is he?" the criminal snapped back.

"But where shall I call him?"

"At his hotel. The College. Don't act so stupid. Ask for long distance and put the call through as fast as you can."

"I will," said Judy and proceeded to make the call. It couldn't come through fast enough to suit her. It was her only chance.

"Hello, Dad! This is Roxy." She spoke quickly so that Dr. Zoller wouldn't have time to answer her. "I'm at home. At the house in Cleveland. I'm calling from there. I came in with a friend of Mother's. Thought it would save you some money. But it seems there are a few bills here that have to be paid and I haven't anything to pay them with and I've forgotten the combination——"

"Hold on there!" Dr. Zoller's furious voice interrupted her over the wire. "I'm giving that information to no one. What's more, you're not——"

But Judy slammed up the receiver. He had been about to say, "You're not Roxy" and she couldn't let Blackie hear that. He had been standing right at her elbow.

"You see, it made him mad!" she said reproachfully. "I guess we'll have to get the money somewhere else."

"Perhaps you can tell me where," Blackie returned in a stinging sarcastic voice.

"Well, the banks open at nine and I have a bank-book."

By nine o'clock, she thought, someone would surely come. Dr. Zoller would know something was wrong and notify the police.

"I don't trust you, little girl," Blackie told her. "There are several things about this business which I don't like at all. That veil over your eyes, for one thing. And the 'Nothing can frighten me' gag for another. I'll have to see this bankbook before I'll believe in it."

"It's in my room," she answered calmly but underneath her breath she begged, "oh, hurry! hurry!" and in the closet where Blackie had shoved her she could hear poor Mrs. Webber beating her knuckles against the door.

"Well, where is your room? Make it snappy."

"How can I find it?" wailed Judy. "I told you I couldn't see."

"I'll find it for you," declared Blackie, shoving ahead of her up the stairs. He flung open the door to one room and discovering a boy's clothing in the closet, quickly closed it again. That must be Terry's room.

Next to it was a larger room with a cushioned window seat and twin beds with a table between them. A pile of school books were stacked on the underneath part of the table.

"This it?" he demanded.

"No-o." Judy spoke slowly as if she could barely see the interior of the room. "That's Helen's and Margie's. Mine's next to it."

She had guessed right for when Blackie flung open the next door she followed him into a room that she knew must belong to Roxy. It was such an individual looking room. The R on the comb, brush and mirror made her more certain. But, now that they had found the room, whatever was she going to do?

Blackie decided that question for her.

"Well, since you can't see, it leaves me the job of finding the bankbook."

And he began throwing open drawer after drawer, spilling the contents on the floor, searching for the bankbook that probably did not exist.

While he was searching, Judy stood as though glued to the floor. Her slightest motion might give away the fact that she could see as clearly as he could. She was tired of playing blind, anyway. She was tired of the tense, desperate feeling that she must be brave when all she wanted to do was to run blindly . . . anywhere . . . away from Blackie.

As she looked around the orderly little room that Blackie was transforming into a place of confusion, Judy noticed the books Roxy read, the kind of perfume she used, the color of her spreads and curtains. Everything harmonized. Even the little pincushion that adorned the dresser was yellow with a brown design. Brown butterflies! Judy stepped nearer, snatched the pincushion and hid it in her pocket.

"What's that you've got?" demanded Blackie, turning sharply.

"I am not afraid. Nothing can frighten me," said Judy in a dangerously quiet voice.

"What's the matter with you? Have you really found something or are you stark, raving crazy? Let's get out of here!"

And he seized her hand and pulled her down the stairs.

"I'm not so sure I'll like holding you for ransom," he told her as they ran. "You'll have me wacky, too."

"Take me where you will. Nothing can frighten me," Judy replied in a spooky monotone.

"Say! You're not trying your father's stunt. I don't fall for it. See? You can't make a sleep-walking idiot out of me—Ouch!" He stumbled over the rug in the hall and nearly fell through the front door. The housekeeper was pounding frantically on the closet door.

"Aren't you going to let Mrs. Webber out of the closet before you leave?" Judy asked him.

"Let her smother!" he growled. "I only wish you were in there with her."

"Why not put me in? I am not afraid. Nothing can frighten me——"

Blackie put his hands to his ears, twisting Judy's arm as he did it.

"For Pete's sake, stop that!" he yelled. "Come on! We're getting out of here!"

"Suits me," Judy replied, groping her way in the bright sunlight which now flooded the porch of Dr. Zoller's home. "When is it going to get daylight?" she asked. "I can't see the car."

Blackie shoved her into it and started off at a furious speed. Judy had no idea where he was heading this time but one thing she did know. Wherever he went, they would have to drive through traffic and she could . . . she must attract someone's attention.

"I've got to do it," she told herself as the car neared a busy corner.

She sat so quietly that Blackie was taken completely by surprise when she suddenly leaned over and grasped the wheel.

Crash! Bang! The street lamp over their heads broke and rained fragments of glass in their faces as the car crashed against the base, then careened in a crazy half circle, nearly running over the traffic cop who stood at the corner.

"Hey you! What's the idea?" yelled the indignant policeman.

"He doesn't know how to drive very well," Judy called sweetly as the car sped on.

Blackie glared at her. "I've a good mind to throw you out of here——"

"I am not afraid," interrupted Judy. "Nothing can frighten me. Nothing at all," she added with new hope as the sound of a police siren screamed behind them.

"You've tricked me!" growled Blackie. "You can see as well as I can."

"You bet I can," Judy replied. "Maybe better. I knew you even though you did try to hide your face when you gave me the pocketbook. But you didn't know me!" And, with that, she removed her hat and veil and fixed her gray-green eyes full upon him. "You see, it isn't Roxy Zoller you're attempting to kidnap. It's Judy Bolton!"

Blackie emitted a sound of rage, stopped the car so short that Judy's forehead struck the windshield with terrific force, and then bolted toward the side of the road.

"He must know something about me," Judy thought dazedly, holding her aching head as she watched him run toward certain capture.

The whole road seemed suddenly bristling with police and radio cars. They were coming from both directions, blurring together, for all at once Judy actually couldn't see. It was her head, she knew. She had given it a terrible crack and, as she felt it, she realized it was cut as well. Probably from the broken street lamp.

In a moment four policemen—and it took that many to subdue him—had Blackie in custody. Judy saw them dimly, heard herself saying something about Mrs. Webber being locked in the closet, and then she knew that the game of pretending, of being Roxy and of being brave when

she was ready to collapse, was over. Closing her
eyes, she slipped down behind the wheel of
Blackie's car and knew nothing more until Peter
tiptoed softly into the living room and she awoke
to find herself at home on the sofa.

CHAPTER XXI

Home Again

"Peter, is that you? I—I thought I was still dreaming," Judy murmured, stirring a little and looking up at him. "It's funny. I thought they captured Blackie. I guess I was hypnotized.'"

"You're all right now," Peter assured her in a quiet voice.

"Then what's this?" she asked feeling the bandage she was now wearing. "Did someone crack me over the head?"

"I'm the one who should have been cracked over the head for letting you into such a mess. But this is the last time, absolutely the last time," Peter declared, "that you go off anywhere chasing crooks without me to protect you."

Judy laughed at that.

"The crooks are the ones who need protection! If this isn't a dream, and I'm beginning to think it isn't," she said, "Blackie was about the most frightened crook I ever happened to meet. I kept telling him nothing could frighten me until he thought I was supernatural, I guess." She giggled. "And all the time he had a gun with him and was afraid to use it. I picked up something in

176

Roxy's room and he thought it was *dangerous*.
Guess what it was, Peter? Only a pincushion!''

"You were alone in Roxy's room with that—
that——''

"Don't say it, Peter," warned Judy. "I'm telling you I frightened him. He didn't dare touch
me. He thought I was—what was it he said? As
crazy as a— No, he said 'stark, raving crazy.'
Glory be! Now I know it wasn't a dream. I remember his very words.''

"Judy, I'll never forgive myself," groaned
Peter. "Suppose something had happened to
you?''

"Are you trying to tell me it didn't? Peter,''
she demanded, sitting up and listening, "who owns
all those voices in the next room?''

"People waiting to congratulate you. A couple
of G-men, a newspaper photographer who, I might
add, has already taken your picture and—'' He
paused impressively. "The great Dr. Zoller.''

"Is Roxy with him?" Judy asked, wide-eyed.

"Yes. Roxy and Helen and Margie and Terry.
The whole family came. Roxy declares that you
saved her life.''

"I guess I did," Judy admitted, "but goodness,
Peter! I wasn't myself. I was the me underneath
—or something," she finished in confusion. "Dr.
Zoller will have to tell you about that. I wouldn't
know.''

"I always knew the you underneath was rather

wonderful,'' Peter said huskily. ''Gosh, Judy! I'd have choked Blackie with my bare hands if I'd been there.''

''Then it's just as well you weren't. I don't believe in violence when strategy works just as well. But, Peter,'' she asked, ''what did happen? Where were all the rest of you while I was having this—this nightmare?''

''We had a few nightmares of our own. Red and I spent most of the time in jail.''

''In jail!'' gasped Judy.

''Yes,'' he replied grimly. ''We committed the crime of breaking and entering. You see, Red ran across Blackie's friend, Button, and who do you think he was?''

''You'll have to tell me. I've done enough guessing.''

''Well, he was none other than the man who gave his name as Kelly and came into the office inquiring about wills. He runs a toy shop in Emporium and we figured he might keep something there besides toys. We weren't so far wrong at that.''

''Go on,'' urged Judy. ''What did you find?''

''Trouble,'' Peter replied, ''and plenty of it. To tell you the truth, Judy, we hadn't had time to look around when the cops burst in on us and took possession of whatever evidence there was. But the hopeful part of it is that they must have found something to prove we were within our rights or we'd still be behind bars.''

"Go on!"

"There isn't any more. Don't you ever get enough? Well, maybe the folks outside can tell you the rest of it. All right!" he called. "You can come in now but, please, not all together."

Judy's mother, pale with worry, was the first to enter.

"Are you all right, dear?" she questioned anxiously. "You can hear me speak?"

"Couldn't I before?"

"Oh, my darling!" Mrs. Bolton sobbed. "We have you back with us. How thankful we all are! You can't imagine how you frightened me."

"I think I can, Mother. I'm sorry," murmured Judy. "You thought I'd been hypnotized, like Lucy, and would never come back again."

"I didn't know what to think. Linda was so happy over being able to sing again that at first she didn't think anything was wrong, but when she did realize that you had taken Roxy's place and kept the appointment with that criminal— Oh, I can't tell you, Judy! We were all so upset and, worst of all, there was nothing that we could do!"

"Well, there is now," Judy told her. "The danger's over, I hope, but there's still so much I don't understand. Mother, what did you think of Dr. Zoller?"

"He seemed quite a respectable gentleman, dear. He and your father have struck up quite a friendship and Linda, naturally, thinks there's no one like him. She wants to come in, dear, and say just a hurried goodbye. She's leaving for her school in an hour.''

Miss Leonard was then ushered in and with her came Dr. Zoller himself. Judy beamed up at them from her cushions.

''Judy, you've been so brave!'' cried the music teacher, her eyes filling with tears of gratitude.

''It isn't exactly brave when you're not afraid, is it?'' asked Judy. ''You see, Linda, you weren't the only person to be hypnotized. I was made quite fearless. I kept repeating what Dr. Zoller told me and it worked. It really did. It made me so brave that I even frightened Blackie.''

''My dear girl,'' Dr. Zoller told her, ''such courage as you displayed was something no hypnotist could have given you. It was already there. You had only to make use of it and, thank Heaven, you did. You realize, of course, that you have saved my daughter's life.''

''Either her life or her money,'' Judy began. ''If she had paid——''

''Judy, please——'' Roxy interrupted, darting through the door.

''Well! Well! What's all the excitement now?'' the doctor asked in surprise, ''I understood the excitement was over with the capture of the kidnapper.''

''You see?'' Roxy's eyes met Judy's and she read in them that there was still something she mustn't tell.

"The excitement is just beginning, I'm afraid," she exclaimed as the rest of her friends burst in to congratulate her. Among them was Mr. Trent. To Judy's astonishment, he had with him the young man who had been following her back in Westlake.

"Meet Mr. Hall," he said. "It was his job to protect you, but unfortunately, he couldn't tell you and your friend apart."

"That's right," agreed the young man, "and do I feel like a dud! Mr. Trent and I had it all planned that I was to follow you and see that Blackie was nabbed the minute he approached you. We had it figured out that you planned to meet him. But our plan slipped up when you and the hypnotist's daughter changed places and, from then on, I kept an eye on her."

"It's just as well you did," Judy told him. "Blackie never suspected that he needed to escape from his intended victim, especially a blind one."

"Blind?"

"Oh, yes. I didn't tell you. I pretended I couldn't see. I had to. I didn't know my way around——"

Mr. Trent chuckled at that. "So you didn't know your way around? The government could use a few more people who are as blind as you and that young lawyer friend of yours."

"You said you didn't need our help," Judy reminded him.

"I confess it. And I didn't take much stock in his theory that there might be another girl who looked like you. Well, I admit my error. Take a look at those two girls, folks, and you may understand why even the housekeeper didn't know them apart."

"Was she all right?" Judy questioned anxiously.

"Suffering from shock and bruised knuckles when the police found her, but otherwise okay and mad as a hornet. Thinks we're lying to her about you not being Roxy."

"With that bandage over your eyes you look still more like her," Peter observed.

"It keeps sliding down," she returned, "and I'm afraid to touch it. Is my head badly hurt?" she asked her father who had just come in. "How did I get here anyway? Did I come in an ambulance? And was I completely wacky?"

"You were delirious, if that's what you mean," Dr. Bolton told her. "As for the bruise on your head, I wouldn't say it was serious. It may leave a small scar."

"Another way to tell us apart," she said, smiling at Roxy. "I wish you could stay here for a day or two," she added. "We didn't really have an opportunity to get acquainted and there is so much I want to tell you. I was in your room, you know."

"I know. And the next time you visit it, I certainly hope it will be on a more pleasant occasion.''

"Look, Roxy!'' Judy took the small pincushion from the pocket of her tan coat which was beside her on the sofa. "I helped myself to this. Do you mind?''

Roxy's blue eyes widened.

"Judy dear, you could have anything—anything but that. That's one of my treasures. I had my whole room done over on purpose to match it.''

"I understand,'' Judy answered slowly, wondering if she did. "I have some treasures too. If you'll stay we can go over to Grandma's house together and I'll show them to you. There's a wonderful patchwork quilt that I'd like especially to have you see.''

"May I?'' Roxy asked her father.

"Certainly, if Judy wants you. After this,'' he said with a bow of gratitude, "the whole Zoller family is hers to command.''

"I may remember that, Dr. Zoller,'' she told him seriously.

CHAPTER XXII

Roxy's Problem

THE two days' vacation from the office which Judy had planned lengthened out into a week. During that time Roxy met most of Judy's friends and was included in their plans for future parties, chief of which was a bridal shower which Lois was planning for Lorraine and Judy who had decided to have a double wedding in June.

March was drawing to a close and its windy, blustery weather made June seem very far away. Still Judy enjoyed planning ahead. Roxy shared her enthusiasm and yet she appeared vaguely troubled about something. She denied it when Judy asked her if it had anything to do with Blackie.

"Why should I worry about him now that he's locked up where he belongs? I always hated the man," Roxy declared. "I used to hide when he came to see Mother. I couldn't bear to see them together. I don't think I ever hated anyone quite so much as I hate him. That's why I'm so grateful to you, Judy. If I had met him—" She shuddered. "Well, I probably would have told him I

184

hated him, but Judy, I wouldn't have bought his information, whatever it was. I didn't intend to do that. I only intended to ask him to leave us alone."

"But you would have paid him, wouldn't you?" Judy questioned.

"No," she declared. "I had another plan. Look!" And she pulled from her purse a small, pearl-handled revolver. "You see, it was only for protection——"

"Oh, Roxy!" burst out Judy, "I'm so glad you didn't meet him. To think what might have happened!"

"A friend of mine loaned me the revolver," Roxy explained. "It's from a collection of fire-arms that her father has. He's away and won't miss it for a week and by then I will have given it back."

"You haven't a permit for it, have you?"

"Goodness, no! I'm scared to death of it but, you see, I couldn't have Blackie telling things— whatever it is he thinks he knows. I only intended to threaten him the way he's threatened us. I suspected all along that he wasn't really an insurance agent."

"But, Roxy, there couldn't be anything so terrible to tell."

"That's what I keep saying to myself," the girl answered. "Whatever it was, I'm sure it was all lies and I wouldn't hear it for the world. I'm glad he didn't tell you. I wouldn't want anybody to hear what he has to say. He didn't mention anything, did he?''

"Nothing more than what was in the note—about a fortune and your folks keeping it from you. It sounded slightly ridiculous to me," Judy said, "for I'm sure your father gives you everything you want."

"He's too generous," Roxy declared. "He and Mother both seemed to treat me better than the other children—as though I were somebody special. But I suppose parents do feel that way about their first child."

"Perhaps they do," Judy agreed. "Horace used to be petted a lot but then he wasn't healthy when he was small. You'd never think it now, would you?"

"Glory, no!" Roxy replied. "The way he raced about with the news of Blackie's capture was positively superhuman. And he certainly saw to it that you got plenty of credit."

"He would! He always manages to get this family on the front page. But the publicity will be good for Peter," she added, "and Horace was kind enough to give prominence to the fact that it was his theory that I might have a double. I wish he'd mentioned something about the possibility that we might be cousins——"

"But there isn't any such possibility," Roxy interrupted, a strange look of fear which puzzled

Judy coming into her eyes. "That's the one thing
that makes me furious, Judy. I'd give anything if
you'd just drop that idea——"

"Anything?" asked Judy. "Even your pincushion?"

"You already have that and if it makes you
happy to carry it around in your pocket, I suppose
I might as well let you do it."

"It isn't as dangerous as that pearl-handled
thing you were carrying around," Judy charged,
"and it may be more useful."

"Useful? How do you mean?" demanded Roxy.

"Well," Judy said, "it's a clue. In fact, it's the
most important clue I have with one exception.
There's a clue in that patchwork quilt I told you
about. Horace left his car in the parking lot in
case I wanted to drive over to Grandma's house
this afternoon and show it to you."

Roxy straightened herself and looked suspiciously at Judy. The two girls had been sitting in
the living room with Blackberry purring between
them on the sofa. But, at Roxy's sudden motion,
the cat jumped down and walked majestically out
of the room.

"Goodbye-ee!" shrieked Horace's parrot in
exact imitation of Judy's voice.

"You're a queer girl, aren't you?" Roxy said.
"You and your black cat and your shrieking parrot may bring me bad luck after all."

"Don't blame me for that parrot," Judy

pleaded. "He's Horace's. He has a habit of calling out, 'Crook! Swindler! Cheat!' and various other such accusations and, for some reason or other, that amuses my brother. The parrot learned to talk from a gangster who used to own him."

Roxy's eyes narrowed. "You know quite a lot of gangsters, don't you?"

"It just happens. I don't invite them to the house if that's what you mean," Judy explained. "But, somehow, I do seem to run into a number of them. This house used to belong to a woman who was a fence for a gang of crooks, but we didn't know it when we moved in. That's really how it all started, and then, with my brother always on the lookout for news and with Peter trying to smash so many rackets—oh, heavens!" she finished. "I can't explain it. But you see how it is. I don't understand why it should bother you."

"It wouldn't. That is, if I were absolutely certain you didn't find out any of this information Blackie was trying to sell. You were awfully interested in it—for a stranger."

"I told you I hoped I might prove that you and I are cousins," Judy reminded her. "I did find out that your whole name is Roxanna and my cousin's name ended in . . . anna on the birth announcement——"

"And who was this Anna's father?" demanded Roxy.

"I don't know. I only know my grandparents disapproved of him——"

"Then he might have been a crook! He might have been Blackie! Can't you see what you're trying to find out about me, Judy? If I did have bad parents, instead of good ones, it would be better for me not to know it. If Blackie was my father— but I can't bear to think of it. I'd hate myself. I'd want to die!"

Her voice had become hysterical. Judy was alarmed.

"Whatever gave you the idea that he might be?" she asked.

"Well, Mother might have been married to him before she met Dad. I know she was afraid he'd tell me something and what else could it have been? But if that's true," Roxy cried out, "then Dad lied to me and I can't trust anybody!"

"But mightn't it have been the other way around?" Judy suggested. "Mightn't it have been your father who was married before and——"

"No!" Roxy interrupted, dabbing tears from her eyes. "I know it wasn't. I've heard Mother speak of the day she brought me home from the hospital and how I looked and everything. Besides, Dad never speaks of the time when I was a very tiny baby. Mother brought me home and took care of me alone."

"You're sure, Roxy?"

"Positive," she said. "Mother was so afraid Blackie would tell me something, I know she must have paid him to keep quiet about it and after she died he thought he could make me pay to find out. Well, I don't want to know it if he's my father! If that fortune he speaks of is anything he has to give me, any of the money he's swindled—and I know it is! The more I think of it, the more sure I am it's true."

She broke off, sobbing and beating her hands against her pocketbook. Judy, remembering the pearl-handled revolver she had inside, took it gently away from her.

"Roxy dear, you'll mess your pocketbook all up, crying on it that way. I'll take it up to my room. You'll find it on top of my dresser."

Inside Judy's dresser was a secret drawer which appeared to be only a panel of wood. Pressing the small button underneath the panel, she caused the drawer to open. Then she slipped the weapon inside and snapped it shut again.

Downstairs she could hear Roxy still sobbing. Poor girl! So that was what she had feared all along! She had believed that Blackie might be her own father and she had loved Dr. Zoller all the more because of that fear.

"And yet," thought Judy, "their eyes are so alike."

In the mirror Judy studied her own gray eyes. Blue eyes were common, she thought, but not blue eyes with what she now called the Zoller expression. She tried on her hat discovering, to her joy, that the veil nearly hid the cross of adhesive tape on her forehead.

"Now," she said to herself, "since Horace is willing to trust me with the runabout, I think I will take Roxy to Dry Brook Hollow. The fresh air will do her good and whatever we find out, it can't be worse than what she's afraid of. Roxy!" she called. "Put on your things. I've decided to risk our lives in Horace's lame Jenny."

"His what?" she called back.

"His excuse for a car," explained Judy. "I'm going to drive it."

"Can you drive?"

"I hope so," Judy answered. "Anyway, they gave me a driver's license."

"The way I feel," Roxy told her when they were both ready to start, "I wouldn't care if you crashed into a telegraph pole and knocked my brains out. I'd rather not think."

"You're going to have something pleasant to think about before this day is over," Judy prophesied, sliding behind the wheel of Horace's lame Jenny, as she called it.

In the pocket of her light tan coat Judy still carried the pincushion she had taken from Roxy's room. If it meant what she thought it meant— But the patchwork quilt would give her the final answer.

Smiling, Judy started backing the car out of the parking lot where Horace kept it. The driver's license, which she carried in her pocketbook, was a recent acquisition and she still felt jittery while at the wheel of a car. Horace's car was so old and battered that a few more bumps couldn't change its appearance. But they might change the appearance of the two girls inside.

"Do you drive?" she asked anxiously of Roxy.

The girl shook her head.

"Well, here goes then," said Judy and they were off for Dry Brook Hollow.

CHAPTER XXIII

JUDY'S SOLUTION

THE old house in Dry Brook Hollow stood as
though waiting for someone to come and live in it
again. Red was there, of course, but he spent little
time in the house. Warm weather was on its way
and that meant the beginning of his busiest season.
He hoped before long to have a greenhouse to keep
him busy with his landscape gardening the year
round.

Judy met him just as she was about to turn the
car into the narrower road that led to her grandmother's house. He was preparing the ground for
spring planting and she observed that the land he
was cultivating was the very piece that would have
been his under the lost will.

"Might as well make it pretty for the crooks
who intend to swindle me out of it," he grumbled.
"Want me to help you with the car, Judy? You
seem to be having trouble."

One wheel of Horace's lame Jenny had slipped
into the ditch at the side of the road as Judy attempted to turn.

"I think I'll just leave it here and walk the rest
of the way," Judy told him. "I've never at-

193

tempted to drive on such a rutty road and wouldn't
trust myself.''

"Your grandfather's wagon wheels tore it up
last summer," Red explained. "That's another
thing about the place that needs fixing. I'm afraid
your friend won't be so pleased with it, Judy.
Maybe she won't think it's much of a fortune—
hardly worth destroying a will and paying a crook
to get hold of——''

"Roxy knows nothing about the will," Judy interrupted furiously. "You've figured things out
all wrong, Red."

"Well, maybe you can do better." He waved
his hand toward the house. "There it is! Find
the will if you think you can. Find anything worth
two hoots in a hollow——''

"Come on," Judy urged Roxy. "He's in a bad
mood. Maybe his coffee wasn't right or he burned
his toast this morning."

"He didn't even speak to me," said Roxy. "I
met him the other day at your house. The least
he could have done was say 'how do you do?' ''

"He's mad about the lost will—mad at himself
mostly," Judy added, "for if he hadn't been
friends with Blackie it might never have been
lost."

"And now he blames me! You see," Roxy continued as the two girls walked on down the little
road toward the farmhouse, "that's the way it
would be with everybody. They'd all blame me

for being his daughter if it was ever known. I can
understand now why Mother was so frightened.
But what did Blackie expect to gain by taking your
grandmother's will?"

"That," said Judy, "is just what I've been wondering. You see, Roxy, if you are my cousin
and if the will isn't found, then half of this property would go to you. That may be the fortune
Blackie wanted to tell you about. Of course, it
isn't really a fortune. It would mean only a couple
of thousand dollars at the most if the place had to
be sold."

"You wouldn't want it sold, would you, Judy?"
Roxy asked.

"No," she declared. "I love it. I want it kept
in the family. With a new coat of paint and a few
repairs it would be the most beautiful place in the
world. Besides," she added softly, "it's been lived
in by people I love. I know that's a sentimental
reason, but it makes the house mean more to me
than any other house ever could mean. So many
people have new houses and they're all alike. They
haven't any soul until people have lived in them a
while. But there, you see what I mean?"

She pointed to a little footprint that appeared
on the cement as they came up the steps at the side
of the porch.

"That was where I stepped in the wet cement
and now the footprint is no bigger than my hand.
This," she continued, turning her key in the lock,

"is the Sunday door for very special guests. Enter, Roxanna!" And Judy made a sweeping bow.

"How quiet it is—and how homelike," Roxy whispered as she stepped inside on the bright rag rug.

"It is, isn't it?" Judy agreed glancing around. Red must have had someone in to clean up the place, for now everything was dusted and there was not a trace of the plaster that had sifted through the whole house when the piece of ceiling fell. The chest which contained the patchwork quilt was pushed back next to the wall and wood was placed in the fireplace ready to make a fire. Judy lit it and warmed her hands before the bright blaze.

"I brought your pincushion along," she announced a moment later, taking it from her pocket and placing it beside her grandmother's sewing basket. "See how nice it looks with all these other old-fashioned things."

"I suppose I'm selfish," Roxy said, "not to want to part with it. I told you, Judy, that you could have anything else. But that pincushion was made out of a piece from my mother's wedding dress. That's why I treasured it."

Judy's eyes shone.

"Roxy! Wait a minute! Hold your breath!" she cried, flinging open her chest. "There!" She placed the patchwork quilt in Roxy's arms.

"What in the world?" the girl exclaimed.

"This!" said Judy, pointing triumphantly to
the piece she had called her clue. "This was
Lucy's wedding dress *and they are the same!* See,
the same yellow cloth and exactly the same brown
butterflies! That's why I wanted your pincushion.
It means we are cousins, Roxy! It couldn't mean
anything else!"

And Judy hugged Roxy, expecting her to share
her joyous enthusiasm. But instead her face became as white as wax.

"Then they both lied. Neither of them are my
real parents. Blackie must have known it! He
must have known your Aunt Lucy was my mother.
And how could he have known that unless she was
married to him? I can't bear it, Judy! Why did
you tell me?"

"Dearest Roxy, don't jump to such awful con-
clusions. Couldn't Lucy have married your
father?"

"But you said your grandparents were against
him. They wouldn't have been against my father!"

"They might have been," Judy said thoughtfully. "Even Mother was horrified when she
learned that I was going to hear a hypnotist. She
just didn't understand."

"But my mother, Edith Terry, brought me home
from the hospital. I've heard her mention it and
I've heard her tell how she nursed me through
scarlet fever when I was only three months old.
I can't believe it wasn't true!"

"Your father might be able to explain it, Roxy."

"I'd never ask him," she cried. "Then I'd have to tell him how frightened Mother was and how she gave money to Blackie. Besides, she asked me to promise that I'd never, never tell him that. I think Blackie threatened to kidnap me if she told him. I know he threatened something terrible and Mother lived in fear of what he would do. But if we just keep still then everything will be the way it was before."

"Everything can't be the way it was before," Judy declared. "Now that we've found out this much, we might as well know the whole truth. Besides, Roxy, if the will isn't found you'd have a right to half of Grandma's property."

"That's right. She was my grandmother, too," Roxy said thoughtfully. "Won't you tell me more about her?"

The next hour passed quickly while Judy told Roxy all about Grandmother Smeed, showed her the precious Wedgwood china, the needle paintings, Grandpa's chessmen and both their pictures as well as the pictures of other relatives. Finally they went up to Judy's room where the plaster had fallen. Everything was in order again but the hole made by the falling plaster was still there. It covered a part of the ceiling and extended below it to about the place where one of the pictures had hung.

"Maybe the picture hook started the plaster

cracking," Roxy suggested. "Mother always used
to say it was better to hang pictures from a mould-
ing."

"I wonder if that is what happened," mused
Judy, climbing up on the head rail of the bed and
studying the hole behind the picture. "This must
have been here quite a while," she observed.
"The plaster is darker and the lath behind it is
broken."

"That's what happens. The picture hook probably broke it."

"I don't think so. I think someone broke it
deliberately—to hide something. Roxy, please
hand me my flash. It's in my coat pocket."

As she took it, Judy made sure of her footing
and then sent a beam of light down into the dark
crevice between the walls.

"Oooo! It looks funny! Sort of mysterious.
Imagine it, Roxy! Nobody has ever seen in here
before. Want to look?"

"I don't see anything but the inside of the wall,"
Roxy said in a disappointed voice as she peered
into the hole.

"Neither do I—yet. But wait! There's something white!"

"It moves!" shrieked Roxy. "It rattles too!"
And she sprang away from the wall so quickly
that the bed on which she and Judy were standing
rolled halfway across the room. Judy attempted
to stop it by grasping the wall, but only succeeded

in knocking her flashlight down behind it. Just then Red's voice yelled at them from downstairs.

"Where's the earthquake this time? Peter's here and wants to come up with me if you girls are finished dropping bombs."

CHAPTER XXIV

Explaining the Past

"I'm going to do some cross-examining," Judy announced as Red came into the room ahead of Peter. "Red, if I ask you some questions, will you promise to tell the truth, the whole truth and nothing but the truth?"

"Sure," he replied, "but what do I know?"

"You know, for one thing, who was in this room the night you and your friends were playing cards."

"You're darned right I do," Red answered vehemently. "Blackie was and I wish now I'd stripped his skin off as well as his coat. I was searching him for that deck of marked cards you found in the sewing machine drawer."

"He didn't like that very well, did he, Red?"

"He liked it better than I did," the hired man confessed ruefully. "To tell you the truth, Judy, that's why I was sleeping here. Blackie put me to sleep with a right to the jaw and the Fowler boys, good kids both of them, continued the search and they say Blackie never made a murmur."

"No wonder. He had nothing to be afraid of then. I thought something like that happened,"

Judy declared. "Blackie knocked down one of the pictures during his scuffle with you, didn't he?"

Red's mouth dropped open.

"How in thunder did you know that?"

"And then," continued Judy, "everything became peaceful. He didn't have the marked cards because he had already hidden them in the sewing machine drawer when he took out the will. But he had to dispose of that too. He had not counted on being searched. So he dropped it through the hole behind the picture."

"You mean that your grandmother's will is in between these walls?" Red questioned, unbelieving. "How do you know?"

"I looked down and saw it," Judy declared, "but something made it move, probably another piece of plaster falling on it. I dropped my flashlight down by accident. That was the bomb you heard."

"Thanks for telling me," grinned Red. "I see where the plasterers start work tomorrow with instructions to rip out this wall clear to the floor. I'll turn the will over to you, Peter, directly I get it out of there." He glanced at Roxy and looked a little sheepish. "I hope you'll excuse me for thinking you had anything to do with it," he added.

"Of course," murmured Roxy, a little dazed by all that was happening.

"Judy, I think I'll let you cross-examine my clients after this," Peter told her. "Sometimes I wonder which of us deserves to be called a lawyer, you or me.''

"You, of course," she laughed back at him. ''You can run the office without me, but I'd be lost in it without you. Did anything important happen today?''

"Mr. Trent came in——''

"Oh dear," she interrupted, ''and I could have gone to the office just as well as not. Nobody would have minded the adhesive tape on my head, I'm sure.''

"I think you and Roxy found out something much more important here.''

"We know where the will is and we know we're cousins——''

"You do!'' ejaculated Peter. ''Well, that takes one big worry off my mind. Now I won't mind telling you what Mr. Trent had to report to me.''

"Go on!'' Judy urged him eagerly.

"Well, he thought I might like to know what the police found in the back of Button's toy shop. I guess you'd like to know too, wouldn't you, Red?''

"Sure would," he agreed, ''since it cost us both a night in jail.''

"For one thing," Peter began, ''there was a toy stamping outfit with flags, soldiers, tanks, airplanes and guns on the stamps. One of the gun stamps was missing but later it was found inside a large, roll-top desk. The G-men who were called in discovered that some of the threatening notes

Blackie had written had been blotted on the desk pad.''

"Did he threaten a great many people?" Roxy asked in surprise.

"It looks as though he made quite a business of it," Peter told her. "At any rate, he had a collection of marriage certificates, birth certificates, and I don't know what else besides a card file of perhaps a hundred names. Under each name, written in a code that Mr. Trent easily deciphered, were bits of information that these people wanted kept quiet. The name Zoller was the last one on the list." He paused to see what effect that had on Roxy; then asked, "Shall I go on?"

"Yes, do," Roxy urged. "As Judy says, now that I know this much, I might as well be told the whole truth. I know that Lucy Smeed was my real mother but what I don't know, what I'm fearfully afraid of, is that Blackie is the man she married."

"You mean that he's your real father? I very much doubt that," Peter answered gravely. "Very much indeed. But I can't prove anything one way or the other from what it said in the files. No information was there except the date of your father and mother's marriage. It was nearly a year after you were born."

"Oh," said Roxy. "Then his files didn't tell me as much as Judy's patchwork quilt."

"No," Judy agreed, "they only told you that you might be adopted while the quilt told you who your real mother was. I don't see how we can find out any more unless we ask your father.''

"I'd never ask him," Roxy repeated. "But, Judy, if you want to do it, I really don't mind. He's coming to take me home tomorrow. You could just tell him about my pincushion and the piece on the quilt and see what he says.''

"Better yet," Judy declared, "I'll show them to him. I'll take the quilt home and you and I can sleep under it tonight.''

The patchwork quilt seemed to have bewitched the girls for that night neither of them could sleep. They talked and talked. And every now and then the light would be snapped on as they discussed the pieces in the quilt.

"I'm beginning to understand how you feel about your grandmother's house," Roxy murmured sleepily at about two in the morning. "I'm so glad you found the will," she added. "I wouldn't want half of your grandmother's property. It wouldn't be fair of me to take it when I never knew her.''

"You know her a little now, don't you?" Judy asked, turning over on her pillow.

"Yes, and it must please her, if she can see us from where she is, to know that we've found each other," Roxy said.

After that the long silence told Judy that her newly found cousin had gone to sleep happy. In the morning, when her father arrived, Roxy greeted him as cheerfully as though she had no fears whatsoever.

Judy told Peter that this was positively the last day of her vacation and reminded him, when he called to say hello in the morning, that he mustn't forget to stop off in Dry Brook Hollow and bring home the will.

"Maybe I can coax Dr. Zoller to stay and hear it read," she added. "Roxy would be pleased, I know."

It wasn't until after their pleasant luncheon together that Judy broached the subject of the quilt. She came into the room with it piled so high in her arms that it covered half her face.

"What's this? Are you going to put us all to bed?" asked Dr. Zoller pleasantly.

"Nothing like that," she laughed. "I just wanted to show you Grandma's memory quilt. It's made up of pieces of the clothes worn by all my relatives. There isn't one of the closest ones left out. Even my aunt and uncle that died have pieces that tell stories about them. This," she pointed out, "was Uncle John's shirt. Miss Leonard was engaged to him, you know. That was the tragedy that had to do with her music."

"An interesting quilt, I'm sure. How is Miss Leonard now?" Dr. Zoller inquired.

"Wonderful. She's teaching again and seems very happy."

"I must call on her sometime. A charming woman," mused the doctor.

"Yes, she is." And Judy now pointed out the piece with the circles of stars. "This was her dress. I guess you know that," she added. "You mentioned it the night of the lecture and so I thought perhaps you had met her before."

"No, I'm sorry to say I never had the pleasure."

"It's strange that you should have known about her dress. But here's something stranger still," said Judy, pointing to the yellow piece with the brown butterflies. "This was my Aunt Lucy's wedding dress. She ran away and married a stranger. Now that Grandma's dead, none of us know who he was. But we do know she had a daughter about the age of Roxy. I found the birth announcement that had been lost."

"And when did you find it?" inquired Dr. Zoller.

"Only a short time ago. Naturally, I began searching for my cousin. Then, when Roxy and I met in the restaurant, I was sure I'd found her because we look so much alike."

Roxy gave a queer little gulp and left the table for a minute. Horace, who was home for lunch, had forgotten he was due back at the office. Dr. Bolton was watching his daughter with a proud light in his eyes while Mrs. Bolton sat on the edge of her chair.

"Well, then what?" prompted Dr. Zoller, his face as expressionless as ever.

"Naturally, I asked her. But she wouldn't listen to me until I—I helped myself to this." And Judy exhibited the pincushion.

"Well?"

"She said it was made out of her mother's wedding dress."

A long silence followed, a tense silence in which everybody seemed to be waiting for someone else to say something. Horace broke it at last.

"Think I'd better get back to the office. The boss'll fire me," he began.

"Wait a minute, boy." Dr. Zoller's voice stopped him. "You may as well give it to the paper, now that you all know. I feel like a bug impaled on one of the pins in that confounded pincushion and it would help me as little to protest. Yes, the pieces are the same. Lucy Smeed was Roxy's mother and," he added impressively, "she was my wife."

CHAPTER XXV

Plans for the Future

"Dad! Oh, Dad!" cried Roxy throwing her arms around him. "I thought I was adopted. I thought maybe some crook was my father, some awful gangster and you were afraid to tell me. But why did you keep it secret all these years?"

"Your mother wanted you to think you were her own baby," Dr. Zoller explained, pushing his chair back from the table and drawing Roxy next to him. "And can you blame her, dear? She was your nurse. Your poor mother never saw you. She was too ill to care whether or not she had a baby and when she died Edith took you and cared for you in her own home until we were married a year later. She was even kinder to you, dear, than she was to her own children. If it hadn't been for you I doubt if she would have married me at all."

"Then it was all true—all the things she told me about when I was a baby? I'm so happy!" breathed Roxy. "Now I don't care who knows that Judy and I are cousins. And Helen and Margie and Terry are my real sisters and brother after all."

"Half sisters and half brother, but you don't
209

need to think of that,'' Dr. Zoller told her. ''Perhaps it was foolish of us to keep it from you, but Edith had a stepmother who was like the cruel stepmothers one reads about in fairy tales. She hated her and she was afraid you'd feel the same way if you knew. She once made me promise that I'd never tell you. Well, I haven't,'' he finished. ''You've found it out for yourself.''

''You mean Judy found it out. She's a detective, Dad. Everybody says so,'' Roxy told him. ''All her friends have been telling me about the wonderful mysteries she's solved, but this is the most wonderful of all. And Dad, only yesterday she found her grandmother's lost will between the walls of the old farmhouse. I never saw anything so clever.''

And Roxy ran on, describing their adventures of the previous day and warning her father that he must not, under any circumstances, leave until Peter had come in with the will.

''The plasterers are taking down the wall today,'' she explained, ''and so he's sure to have it by the time he comes home.''

Horace had to leave for the office with his news as an excuse for being late. Dr. Bolton received a call from one of his patients. But Judy and Roxy and Mrs. Bolton visited with Dr. Zoller all afternoon. He explained how he knew about Miss Leonard's dress. Lucy had told him about the night her friend first sang in the choir and even described her clothes. The name, Linda Leonard, was familiar to him long before they met.

"Allowing her to believe she was wearing that dress created an atmosphere far removed from the present," Dr. Zoller said, "and that is what I desired. I had no intention of making anyone believe I had any supernatural powers."

"You've been a hypnotist a long time, haven't you?" asked Mrs. Bolton.

"Yes," he admitted. "I worked my way through medical school practicing hypnotism in a circus side show. Lucy used to steal away from home in order to watch it and I thought it unfair of her family not to allow her to see me. Now I would have solved the problem simply by inviting them to one of my demonstrations."

"You've certainly shown me the good there is in it," Mrs. Bolton declared. "I was as prejudiced as my parents ever were before you worked this miracle on Linda. Now the doctor will know where to send his incurable patients——"

"I can't always promise miracles, Mrs. Bolton," he reminded her kindly.

"This was certainly one. Judy dear, you must have Roxy come and visit us often."

"I will. Oh, Mums!" Judy cried out, starting up from the sofa and stepping on Blackberry's tail in her haste to reach the front door. "There's Peter and he has the will!"

The young lawyer came in all smiles exhibiting,

not only the will, but Judy's flashlight as well.   He was eager to hear all the latest developments but refused to break the seal on the will until that evening when every member of the family was present.   Naturally, Red had to be on hand and even Linda was called for and sat with the family as the will was finally opened.

Peter began reading in a clear but solemn voice:

"I, Melissa Smeed, being of sound mind and memory, do hereby declare this to be my last will and testament, hereby revoking all former wills by me made.

"To my granddaughter, Judy Bolton, I hereby give and bequeath all real and personal property . . ."

But here Judy's eyes filled with tears of gratitude.   She hardly listened to the rest of the will.   All real and personal property meant the house, the dear house with all its wonderful past, with all its dreams of the future.   All the things in it were to be hers—hers— She could hardly believe it.   She and Peter would live there.   It would be their home in the country.   No matter where they traveled, no matter what happened, they would always come back to it.   The family Thanksgivings, the family Christmases would be the same.   It was too much—too much— She almost felt that she did not deserve it.

But Horace was not left out.   The wood lot was his, the hillside where as children and as growing young people they had picnicked, the cave with the underground river. All the land across the road was Horace's with the exception of the piece she had left to Red.

"Dearest children," Mrs. Bolton said when Peter had finished reading, "your grandmother knew that nothing would make me as happy as seeing you happy. She was so thoughtful, even marking the treasures in the chest for the people she thought ought to have them. But now, there's one more gift—something your grandmother didn't mention. The patchwork quilt."

"But it's yours, Mother—" Judy began.

"No, dear, I couldn't accept it. I think it ought to belong to Roxy. The rest of us have lived those memories. We have them with us. But Roxy has nothing except the story in the quilt."

"Oh, but I have!" cried Roxy. "I have an aunt, an uncle, two cousins and a house where I know I shall often be invited."

"You are already," Judy told her. "You're invited for next Christmas. Peter and I will be married by then and we want the grandest family gathering."

"Indeed we do," declared Peter. "Your father and the other children are invited too."

"And what about this house?" asked Dr. Bolton with a twinkle in his eye. "Is nobody going to come to it any more?"

"Oh, Dad! You old dear. We'll never let you and Mother be lonely," Judy promised. "We're going to be the happiest, happiest family. How long do you suppose it will take to fix up the house? Will it be finished by June?"

"The wedding date?" questioned Roxy. "I have to keep all these dates straight in my mind."

"I haven't quite straightened them out myself," Judy admitted. "I haven't had time to think about a wedding."

"I do believe, dear," Mrs. Bolton told her, "that your grandmother meant you and Peter to have the house as a wedding gift. She knew you'd live in it while none of the rest of us could have done so—and she did want her house to have people in it."

"It will have, Mother. And isn't it the wonderfullest, wonderfullest gift!"

It was so wonderful, in fact, that Judy had to invent a few more words to describe it. But, while the house might be the most wonderful gift she would receive, it would not be the strangest. Long before June and the proposed wedding date, Judy would be attempting to solve the mystery of THE MARK ON THE MIRROR. But she knew nothing of that now and her eyes were shining with joy as she turned to Peter.

"Our house, our very own house," she whispered softly. "Now we can really begin making plans for the future."

Printed in the United States
119364LV00004B/25-51/P